"Is it time for me to bring in more sheep?" Lizzie asked.

"It's time for a rest and some lunch."

She grimaced as she rubbed her hands together. "I had no idea their wool could be so greasy."

"It's lanolin. It gives you soft skin." Carl held out his hand. She ran her fingers across his palm. He inhaled sharply as his heart beat faster.

She must've sensed something, because her gaze locked with his. He wanted more than the brief touch of her fingers. He wanted to hold her hand. To reach out and pull her close. He wanted to learn everything there was to know about this amazing woman.

She quickly turned away. "I'd better get something ready for lunch. I hope cold sandwiches will be okay."

"That will be fine."

"Goot."

He watched her hurry away and wished he had a reason to call her back.

Books by Patricia Davids

Love Inspired

His Bundle of Love
Love Thine Enemy
Prodigal Daughter
The Color of Courage
Military Daddy
A Matter of the Heart
A Military Match
A Family for Thanksgiving
*Katie's Redemption
*The Doctor's Blessing
*An Amish Christmas
*The Farmer Next Door
*The Christmas Quilt
*A Home for Hannah
*A Hope Springs Christmas
*Plain Admirer
*Amish Christmas Joy
*The Shepherd's Bride

*Brides of Amish Country

Love Inspired Suspense

A Cloud of Suspicion
Speed Trap

PATRICIA DAVIDS

After thirty-five years as a nurse, Pat has hung up her stethoscope to become a full-time writer. She enjoys spending her new free time visiting her grandchildren, doing some long-overdue yard work and traveling to research her story locations. She resides in Wichita, Kansas. Pat always enjoys hearing from her readers. You can visit her on the web at www.patriciadavids.com.

The Shepherd's Bride
Patricia Davids

HARLEQUIN® LOVE INSPIRED®

Recycling programs for this product may not exist in your area.

™ LOVE INSPIRED BOOKS

ISBN-13: 978-0-373-87877-2

THE SHEPHERD'S BRIDE

www.Harlequin.com

Printed in U.S.A.

He shall feed his flock like a shepherd: he shall gather the lambs with his arm, and carry them in his bosom, and shall gently lead those that are with young.

—*Isaiah* 40:11

This book is dedicated with endearing love to my lambs, Kathy, Josh and Shantel.

Chapter One

"You can't be serious." Lizzie Barkman gaped at her older sister, Clara, in shock.

Seated on the edge of the bed in the room the four Barkman sisters shared, Clara kept her eyes downcast. "It's not such a bad thing."

Lizzie fell to her knees beside Clara and took hold of her icy hands. "It's not a bad thing. It's a horrible thing. You can't marry Rufus Kuhns. He's put two wives in the ground already. Besides, he's thirty years older than you are."

"Onkel wishes this."

"Then our uncle is crazy!"

Clara glanced fearfully at the door. "Hush. Do not earn a beating for my sake, sister."

Lizzie wasn't eager to feel the sting of their uncle's wooden rod across her back, but it was outrageous to imagine lovely, meek Clara paired with such an odious man. "Tell Onkel Morris you won't do it."

"He won't go against Rufus's wishes. He's too scared of losing our jobs and this house."

It was true. Their uncle wouldn't oppose Rufus. He didn't have the courage. Rufus Kuhns was a wealthy member of their small Plain community in northern Indiana. He owned the dairy farm where they all worked for the paltry wages he paid. He claimed that letting them live in the run-down house on his property more than made up for their low salaries. The house was little more than a hovel, although the girls tried their best to make it a home.

"Onkel says it is his duty to see us all wed. I'm twenty-five with no prospects. I'm afraid he is right about that."

The single women in their isolated Amish community outnumbered the single men three to one. Lizzie was twenty-three with no prospects in sight, either. Who would her uncle decide she should marry?

"Being single isn't such a bad thing, Clara. Look at my friend Mary Miller, the schoolteacher. She is happy enough."

Clara managed a smile. "It's all right, Lizzie. At least this way I have the hope of children of my own. If God wills it."

It hurt to see Clara so ready to accept her fate. Lizzie wouldn't give up so easily. "Rufus had no children with his previous wives. You don't have to do this. We can move away and support ourselves by making cheese to sell to the tourists. We'll grow old together and take care of each other."

Clara cupped Lizzie's cheek. "You are such a dreamer. What will happen to our little sisters if we do that?"

Greta and Betsy were outside finishing the evening milking. At seventeen, Betsy was the youngest. Greta was nearly twenty. They all worked hard on the dairy farm. With twenty-five cows to be milked by hand twice a day, there was more than enough work to go around. Without Clara and Lizzie to carry their share of the load, the burden on their sisters would double, for their uncle wouldn't pick up the slack.

Morris Barkman hadn't been blessed with children. He and his ailing wife took in his four nieces when their parents died in a buggy accident ten years before. He made no secret of the fact that his nieces were his burden to bear. He made sure everyone knew how generous he was and how difficult his life had been since his wife's passing.

Lizzie couldn't count the number of times she had been forced to hold her tongue when he shamed her in front of others for her laziness and ingratitude. Her uncle claimed to be a devout member of the Amish faith, but in her eyes, he was no better than the Pharisees in the Bible stories the bishop preached about during the church services.

She rose and paced the small room in frustration. There had to be a way out of this. "We can all move away and get a house together. Greta and Betsy, too."

"If we left without our uncle's permission, we would be shunned by everyone in our church. I could not bear that." Clara's voice fell to a whisper. "Besides, if I won't wed Rufus…Betsy is his second choice."

Lizzie gasped. "She's barely seventeen."

"You see now why I have to go through with it. Promise me you won't tell her she's the reason I'm doing this."

"I promise."

"I know you've been thinking about leaving us, Lizzie. I'm not as strong as you are. I can't do it, but you should go. Go now while you have the chance. I can bear anything if I know you are safe."

Lizzie didn't deny it. She had been thinking about leaving for years. She had even squirreled away a small amount of money for the day. Only the thought of never seeing her sisters again kept her from taking such a drastic step. She loved them dearly.

The bedroom door opened and the two younger Barkman girls came in. Greta was limping. Clara immediately went to her. "What happened?"

"She got kicked by that bad-tempered cow we all hate," Betsy said.

"She's not bad-tempered. She doesn't hear well. I startled her. It was my own fault. It's going to leave a bruise, but nothing is broken." Greta sat on the edge of the bed she shared with Betsy.

Clara insisted on inspecting her leg. It was already swollen and purple just above the knee. "Oh, that must hurt. I'll get some witch hazel for it."

As Clara left, Lizzie turned to her sisters. "Onkel is making Clara marry Rufus Kuhns."

"Are you joking? He's ancient." Greta looked as shocked as Lizzie was.

"It's better than being an old *maedel,*" Betsy said. "We're never going to find husbands if we aren't allowed to attend singings and barn parties in other Amish communities."

Would she feel the same if she knew how easily she could trade places with Clara? Lizzie kept silent. She had given Clara her word. Betsy began to get ready for the night.

Greta did the same. "Rufus is a mean fellow."

Lizzie turned her back to give her sisters some privacy. "He's cruel to his horses and his cattle. I can't bear to think of Clara living with him."

"His last wife came to church with a bruised face more than once. She claimed she was accident-prone, but it makes a person wonder." Greta pulled on her nightgown.

"Shame on you, Greta. It's a sin to think evil thoughts about the man." Betsy climbed into bed, took off her black *kapp* and started to unwind her long brown hair.

Greta and Lizzie shared a speaking glance but kept silent. Neither of them wanted their oldest sister to find out if their suspicions were true. They remembered only too well the bruises their mother bore in silence when their father's temper flared.

Clara returned with a bottle of witch hazel and a cloth. "This will help with the pain."

Greta took the bottle from her. They had all used the remedy on bruises inflicted by their uncle over the years. He wouldn't stand up to Rufus, but he didn't have any qualms about taking his anger and frustration out on someone weaker. "You can't do it, Clara. You should go away."

"And never see you again? How could I do that? Besides, where would I go? We have no family besides each other."

Lizzie met Greta's eyes. Greta gave a slight nod. After all, they were desperate. Lizzie said, "We have a grandfather."

"We do?" It was Betsy's turn to look shocked as she sat up in bed.

Clara shook her head. "*Nee.* He is dead to us."

"He is dead to Uncle Morris, not to me." Lizzie's mind began to whirl. Would their *daadi* help? They hadn't heard from him in years. Not since the death of their parents.

Greta rubbed the witch hazel on her knee. "We were told never to mention him."

"Mention who?" Betsy almost shouted.

They all hushed her. None of the sisters wished to stir their uncle's wrath. "Our mother's father lives in Hope Springs, Ohio."

Clara began getting ready for bed, too. "You think he does. He could be dead for all we know."

"We really have a grandfather? Why haven't I met him?" Betsy looked as if she might burst into tears.

Lizzie removed the straight pins that held her faded

green dress closed down the front. "We moved away from Hope Springs when you were just a baby."

Clara slipped under the covers. "Papa and Grandfather Shetler had a terrible falling out when I was ten. Mama, Papa, Uncle Morris and his wife all moved away and eventually settled here."

"Grandfather raised sheep." Lizzie smiled at the memory of white lambs leaping for the sheer joy of it in green spring pastures. She hated it when her father made them move to this dreary place. She hung her dress beside her sisters' on the pegs that lined the wall and slipped into her nightgown.

"Do we have a grandmother, too?" Betsy asked.

Lizzie shook her head. "She died when our mother was a baby. I'm ready to put out the lamp. You know how Onkel hates it when we waste kerosene.

"Grandfather had a big white dog named Joker," Greta added wistfully. "I'm sure he's gone by now. Dogs don't live that long."

"But men do. I will write to him first thing in the morning and beg him to take you in, Clara." Lizzie sat down on her side of the bed and blew out the kerosene lamp, plunging the small bedroom into darkness.

Clara sighed. "This is crazy talk. Our uncle will forbid such a letter, Lizzie. You know that. Besides, I'm not going anywhere without my sisters."

Lizzie waited until Clara was settled under the covers with her. Quietly, she said, "You will go to Rufus Kuhns's home without us."

"I...know. I miss Mama so much at times like this."

Lizzie heard the painful catch in her sister's voice. She reached across to pull Clara close. "I do, too. I refuse to believe she made your beautiful star quilt for this sham of a marriage. She made your quilt to be her gift to you on a happy wedding day."

Their mother had lovingly stitched wedding quilts for each of her daughters. They lay packed away in the cedar chest in the corner. The quilts were different colors and personalized for each one of them. They were cherished by the girls as reminders of their mother's love.

Lizzie hardened her resolve. "We'll think of something. It's only the middle of March. We have until the wedding time in autumn. You'll see. We'll think of something before then."

"*Nee*. My wedding will take place the first week of May so I may help with spring planting."

Greta slipped into bed behind Lizzie. "That's not right. We can't prepare for a wedding in such a short time."

"Rufus doesn't want a big wedding. It will be only the bishop, Uncle Morris, you girls and Rufus."

Such a tiny, uncelebrated affair wasn't the wedding dream of any young woman. Lizzie felt the bed sag again and knew Betsy had joined them on the other side of Clara.

"I don't want you to leave us." Betsy's voice trembled as she spoke.

"I won't be far away. Why, you'll all be able to come for a visit whenever you want."

A visit. That was it! A plan began to form in Lizzie's mind. She was almost certain she had enough money saved to travel to Ohio on the bus. Their grandfather might ignore a letter, but if she went to see him in person, she could make him understand how dire the situation was.

It was an outrageous plan, but what choice did she have? None.

Clara couldn't marry Rufus. He would crush her gentle spirit and leave her an empty shell. Or worse.

Lizzie bit her bottom lip. She couldn't let that happen.

Nor could she tell her sisters what she intended to do. She didn't want them to lie or cover for her. As much as it hurt, she would have to let them think she had run away.

Her younger sisters soon returned to their own bed. Before long, their even breathing told Lizzie they were asleep. Clara turned over and went to sleep, too.

Lizzie lay wide-awake.

If she went through with her plan, the only person she dared tell was Mary Miller. There was no love lost between the schoolteacher and their uncle. Besides, it wasn't as if Lizzie was leaving the Amish. She was simply traveling to another Amish community. If she wrote to her friend from Ohio, she was certain that Mary would relay messages to the girls. If their grandfather proved willing to take them in, Mary would help them leave.

Lizzie pressed her hand to her mouth. Would it work? Could she do it?

If she went, it would have to be tonight while the others were asleep. Before she lost her nerve. She closed her eyes and folded her hands.

Please, Lord, let this plan be Your will. Give me the strength to see it through.

She waited until it was well after midnight before she slipped from beneath the covers. The full moon outside cast a band of pale light across the floor. It gave her enough light to see by. She carefully withdrew an envelope with her money from beneath the mattress and pulled an old suitcase from under the bed. It took only five minutes to gather her few belongings. Then she moved to the cedar chest.

Kneeling in front of it, she lifted the lid. Clara's rose-and-mauve star quilt lay on top. Lizzie set it aside and pulled out the quilt in shades of blue and green that was to be her wedding quilt. Should she take it with her?

If she did, it would convince everyone she wasn't returning. If she left it, her sisters would know she was coming back.

Suddenly, Lizzie knew she couldn't venture out into the unknown without something tangible of her family to bring her comfort. She replaced Clara's quilt and softly closed the lid of the cedar chest.

Holding her shoes, her suitcase and her quilt, Lizzie tiptoed to the door of their room. She opened it with a trembling hand and glanced back at her sisters sleeping quietly in the darkness. Could she really go through with this?

Carl King scraped most of the mud off his boots and walked up to the front door of his boss's home. Joe Shetler had gone to purchase straw from a neighbor, but he would be back soon. After an exhausting morning spent struggling to pen and doctor one ornery and stubborn ewe, Carl had rounded up half the remaining sheep and moved them closer to the barns with the help of his dog, Duncan.

Tired, with his tongue lolling, the black-and-white English shepherd walked beside Carl toward the house. Carl reached down to pat his head. "You did good work this morning, fella. We'll start shearing them soon if the weather holds."

The sheep needed to spend at least one night inside the barn to make sure their wool was dry before being sheared. Damp wool would rot. There wasn't enough room in the barn for all two hundred head at once. The operation would take three to four days if all went well.

It was important to shear the ewes before they gave birth. If the weather turned bad during the lambing season, many of the shorn ewes would seek shelter in the sheds and barn rather than have their lambs out in the open where the wet and cold could kill the newborns. Having a good lamb crop was important, but Carl knew things rarely went off without a hitch.

Duncan ambled toward his water dish. At the moment, all Carl wanted was a hot cup of coffee. Joe always left a pot on the back of the stove so Carl could help himself.

He opened the front door and stopped dead in his tracks. An Amish woman stood at the kitchen sink. She had her back to him as she rummaged for something. She hadn't heard him come in.

He resisted the intense impulse to rush back outside. He didn't like being shut inside with anyone. He fought his growing discomfort. This was Joe's home. This woman didn't belong here.

"What are you doing?" he demanded. Joe didn't like anyone besides Carl in his house.

She shrieked and jumped a foot as she whirled around to face him. She pressed a hand to her heaving chest, leaving a patch of white soapsuds on her faded green dress. "You scared the life out of me."

He clenched his fists and stared at his feet. "I didn't mean to frighten you. Who are you and what are you doing here?"

"Who are you? You're not Joseph Shetler. I was told this was Joseph's house."

He glanced up and saw the defiant jut of her jaw. He folded his arms over his chest and pressed his lips into a tight line. He didn't say a word as he glared at her.

She was a slender little thing. The top of her head wouldn't reach his chin unless she stood on tiptoe. She was dressed Plain in a drab faded green calf-length dress with a matching cape and apron. She wore dark stockings and dark shoes. Her hair, on the other hand, was anything but drab. It was ginger-red and wisps of it curled near her temples and along her forehead. The rest was hidden beneath the black *kapp* she wore. Her eyes were an unusual hazel color with flecks of gold in their depths.

He didn't recognize her, but she could be a local. He made a point of avoiding people, so it wasn't surprising that he didn't know her.

She quickly realized he wasn't going to speak until she had answered his questions. She managed a nervous smile. "I'm sorry. My name is Elizabeth Barkman. People call me Lizzie. I'm Joe's granddaughter from Indiana. I was just straightening up a little while I waited for him to get home."

As far as Carl knew, Joe didn't have any family. "Joe doesn't have a granddaughter, and he doesn't like people in his house." He shoved his hands into his pockets as the need to escape the house left them shaking.

"Actually, he has four granddaughters. I can see why he doesn't like to have people in. This place is a mess. He certainly could use a housekeeper. I know an excellent one who is looking for a position."

Carl glanced around Joe's kitchen. It was cluttered and dirty, unlike the clean and sparsely furnished shepherd's hut out in the pasture where he lived, but if Joe wanted to live like this, that was his business and not the business of this nosy, pushy woman. "This is how Joe likes it. You should leave."

"Where is my grandfather? Will he be back soon?" Her eyes darted around the room. He could see fear creeping in behind them. It had dawned on her that they were alone together on a remote farm.

Suddenly, he saw another room, dark and full of women huddled together. He could smell the fear in the air. They were all staring at him.

He blinked hard and the image vanished. His heart started pounding. The room began closing in on him. He needed air. He needed out. He'd seen enough fear in women's eyes to haunt him for a lifetime. He didn't need to add to that tally. He took a quick step back. "Joe will be along shortly." Turning, he started to open the door.

She said, "I didn't catch your name. Are you a friend of my grandfather's?"

He paused and gripped the doorknob tightly so she wouldn't see his hand shaking. "I'm Carl King. I work here." He walked out before she could ask anything else.

Once he was outside under the open sky, his sense of panic receded. He drew a deep, cleansing breath. His tremors grew less with each gulp of air he took. His pounding heart rate slowed.

It had been weeks since one of his spells. He'd started to believe they were gone for good, that perhaps God had forgiven him, but Joe's granddaughter had proved him wrong.

His dog trotted to his side and nosed his hand. He managed a little smile. "I'm okay, Duncan."

The dog whined. He seemed to know when his master was troubled. Carl focused on the silky feel of the dog's thick fur between his fingers. It helped ground him in the here and now and push back the shadows of the past.

That past lay like a beast inside him. The terror lurked, ready to spring out and drag him into the nightmares he suffered through nearly every night. He shouldn't be alive. He should have accepted death with peace in his heart, secure in the knowledge of God's love and eternal salvation. He hadn't.

He had his life, for what it was worth, but no peace.

Joe came into sight driving his wagon and team of draft horses. The wagon bed held two dozen bales of straw. He pulled the big dappled gray horses to a stop beside Carl. "Did you get that ewe penned and doctored?"

"I did."

"*Goot*. We'll get this hay stored in the big shed so we can have it handy to spread in the lambing pens when we need it. We can unload it as soon as I've had a bite to eat and a cup of coffee. Did you leave me any?"

"I haven't touched the pot. You have a visitor inside."

A small elderly man with a long gray beard and a dour expression, Joe climbed down from the wagon slowly. To Carl's eyes, he had grown frailer this past year. A frown creased his brow beneath the brim of the flat-topped straw hat he wore. He didn't like visitors. "Who is it?"

"She claims she's your granddaughter Lizzie Barkman."

All the color drained from Joe's face. He staggered backward until he bumped into the wheel of his wagon. "One of my daughter's girls? What does she want?"

Carl took a quick step toward Joe and grasped his elbow to steady him. "She didn't say. Are you okay?"

Joe shook off Carl's hand. "I'm fine. Put the horses away."

"Sure." Carl was used to Joe's brusque manners.

Joe nodded his thanks and began walking toward the house with unsteady steps. Carl waited until he had gone inside before leading the team toward the corral at the side of the barn. He'd worked with Joe for nearly four years. The old man had never mentioned he had a daughter and granddaughters.

Carl glanced back at the house. Joe wasn't the only one who kept secrets. Carl had his own.

Chapter Two

Lizzie had rehearsed a dozen different things to say when she first saw her grandfather, but his hired man's abrupt appearance had rattled her already frayed nerves. When her grandfather actually walked through the door, everything she had planned to say left her head. She stood silently as he looked her up and down.

He had changed a great deal from what she remembered. She used to think he was tall, but he was only average height and stooped with age. His beard was longer and streaked with gray now. It used to be black.

Nervously, she gestured toward the sink. "I hope you don't mind that I washed a few dishes. You have hot water right from the faucet. It isn't allowed in our home. Our landlord says it's worldly, but it makes doing the dishes a pleasure."

"You look just like your grandmother." His voice was exactly as she remembered.

She smiled. "Do I?"

"It's no good thing. She had red hair like yours. She was an unhappy, nagging woman. Why have you come? Have you brought sad news?"

"Nee," Lizzie said quickly. "My sisters are all well.

We live in Indiana. Onkel Morris and all of us work on a dairy farm there."

Joe moved to the kitchen table and took a seat. "Did your uncle send you to me? He agreed to raise the lot of you. He can't change his mind now."

She sat across from him. "*Nee,* Onkel does not know I have come to see you."

"How did you get here?"

"I took the bus. I asked about you at the bus station in Hope Springs. An Amish woman waiting to board the bus told me how to find your farm. I walked from town."

He propped his elbows on the table and pressed his hands together. She noticed the dirt under his fingernails and the calluses on his rough hands. "How is it that you have come without your uncle's knowledge? Do you still reside with him or have you married?"

"None of us are married. Onkel Morris would have forbidden this meeting had he known of my plan."

"I see." He closed his eyes and rested his chin on his knuckles.

She didn't know if he was praying or simply waiting for more of an explanation. She rushed ahead, anxious that he hear exactly why she had made the trip. "I had to come. You are the only family we have. We desperately need your help. Onkel Morris is forcing Clara to marry a terrible man. I fear for her if she goes through with it. I'm hoping—praying really—that you can find it in your heart to take her in. She is a good cook and she will keep your house spotless. Your house could use a woman's touch. Clara is an excellent housekeeper and as sweet-tempered as anyone. You must let her come. I'm begging you."

He was silent for so long that she wondered if he had fallen asleep the way old people sometimes did. Finally, he spoke. "My daughter chose to ignore my wishes in order to marry your father. She made it clear that he was more important than my feelings. I can only honor what I believe to be her wishes. I will not aid you in your disobedience to the man who has taken your father's place. You have come a long way for no reason. Carl will take you back to the bus station."

Lizzie couldn't believe her concerns were being dismissed out of hand. "Daadi, I beg you to reconsider. I did not come here lightly. I truly believe Clara is being sentenced to a life of misery, or worse."

Joe rose to his feet. "Do not let your girlish emotions blind you to the wisdom of your elders. It is vain and prideful to question your uncle's choice for your sister."

"It is our uncle who is blind if he thinks Clara will be happy with his choice. She won't be. He is a cruel man."

"If your uncle believes the match is a good thing, you must trust his judgment. There will be a bus going that way this afternoon. If you hurry, you can get a seat. Go home and beg his forgiveness for your foolishness. All will be well in the end, for it is as Gott wills."

"Please, Daadi, you have to help Clara."

He turned away and walked out the door, leaving Lizzie speechless as she stared after him.

Dejected, she slipped into her coat and glanced around the cluttered kitchen. If only he would realize how much better his life would be with Clara to care for him.

Was he right? Was her failure God's will?

With a heavy heart, she carried her suitcase and the box with her quilt in it out to the front porch. Her grandfather was nowhere in sight, but his hired man was leading a small white pony hitched to a cart in her direction.

He was a big, burly man with wide shoulders and narrow hips. He wore a black cowboy hat, jeans and a flannel shirt under a stained and worn sheepskin jacket. His hair was light brown and long enough to touch his collar, but it was clean. His size and stealth had frightened the wits out of her in the house earlier. Out in the open, he didn't appear as menacing, but he didn't smile and didn't meet her gaze.

He and her grandfather must get along famously with few words spoken and never a smile between them.

It was all well and good to imagine staying until her grandfather changed his mind, but the reality was much different. He had ordered her to go home. How could she make him understand if he wouldn't hear what she had to say? He hadn't even offered the simple hospitality of his home for the night. He wanted her gone as quickly as possible. She would have to go home in defeat unless she could find some way to support herself and bring her sisters to Hope Springs. She didn't know where to start. All her hopes had been pinned on her grandfather's compassion. Sadly, he didn't have any.

Carl stopped in front of the house and waited for her. She bit her lower lip. Was she really giving up so easily? "Where is my grandfather?"

"He's gone out to the pasture to move the rest of his sheep."

"When will he be back?"

"Hard to say."

"I'd like to speak to him again."

"Joe told me to take you to the bus station. It's plain to me that he was done talking."

She stamped her foot in frustration. "You don't understand. I can't go home."

He didn't say anything. He simply waited beside the pony. A brick wall would have shown more compassion. Defeated by his stoic silence, she descended the steps. He took her bag from her hand and placed it behind the seat of the cart. He reached for the box that contained her quilt and she reluctantly handed it over.

He waited until she had climbed aboard, then he took his place beside her on the wooden seat. With a flip of the reins, he set the pony in motion. She looked back once. The house, which had looked like a sanctuary when she first saw it, looked like the run-down farmstead it truly was. Tears stung her eyes. She tried not to let them fall, but she couldn't hold back a sniffle. She wiped her nose on the back of her sleeve.

Carl cringed at the sound of Lizzie's muffled sniffling. He would have been okay if she hadn't started crying.

He didn't want to involve himself in her troubles. Whatever it was, it was none of his business. He glanced her way and saw a tear slip down her cheek. She quickly wiped it away. She looked forlorn huddled on the seat next to him, like a lost lamb that couldn't find the flock.

He looked straight ahead. "I'm sorry things didn't turn out the way you wanted with your grandfather."

"He's a very uncaring man."

"Joe is okay."

"I'm glad you think so."

"He doesn't cotton to most people."

"I'm not most people. I'm his flesh and blood. He doesn't care that his own granddaughter is being forced into marriage with a hateful man."

Carl looked at her in surprise. "You're being forced to marry someone not of your choosing?"

"Not me. My sister Clara. Our uncle, my mother's brother, took us in after our parents died. Onkel Morris is making Clara marry a man more than twice her age."

"Amish marriages are not arranged. Your sister cannot be compelled to marry against her will."

"The man who wishes to marry Clara is our landlord and employer. He could turn us all out of his house to starve. My uncle is afraid of him." She crossed her arms over her chest.

"But you are not." He glanced at her with respect. It had taken a lot of courage for her to travel so far.

"I'm afraid of him, too. Sometimes, I think he enjoys making life miserable for others." Her voice faded away. She sniffled again.

The pony trotted quickly along the road as Carl pondered Lizzie's story. He had no way to help her and no words of wisdom to offer. Sometimes, life wasn't fair.

After a few minutes, she composed herself enough to ask, "Do you know of anyone who might want to hire a maid or a housekeeper?"

"No." He didn't go into town unless he had to. He didn't mingle with people.

"I would take any kind of work."

"There's an inn in town. They might know of work for you."

She managed a watery smile for him. "*Danki*. Something will turn up."

She was pretty when she smiled. Although her eyes were red-rimmed now, they were a beautiful hazel color. They shimmered with unshed tears in the afternoon light. Her face, with its oval shape, pale skin and sculpted high cheekbones, gave her a classical beauty, but a spray of freckles across her nose gave her a fresh, wholesome look that appealed to him.

It felt strange to have a woman seated beside him. It had been a long time since he had enjoyed the companionship of anyone other than Joe. Did she know he had been shunned? Joe should have told her. Carl wasn't sure how to bring up the subject.

He sat stiffly on the seat, making sure he didn't touch her. If she were unaware of his shunning, he would see that she didn't inadvertently break the tenets of her faith. The sharp, staccato *clip-clop* of the pony's hooves on the blacktop, the creaking of the cart and Lizzie's occasional sniffles were the only sounds in the awkward silence until he crested the hill. A one-room Amish schoolhouse sat back from the road, and the cheerful sounds of children playing during recess reached him. A game of softball was under way.

One little girl in a blue dress and white *kapp* waved to him from her place in the outfield. He waved back when he recognized her. Joy Mast immediately dropped her over-size ball glove and ran toward him. He pulled the pony to a stop. Two boys from the other team ran after her.

"Hi, Carl. How is Duncan? Is he with you today?" She reached the cart and hung on to the side to catch her breath.

He relaxed as he grinned at her. He could be himself around Amish children. They hadn't been baptized and wouldn't be required to shun him. Joy had Down syndrome. Her father, Caleb Mast, had recently returned to the area and rejoined his Amish family. "Hello, Joy. Duncan is fine, but he is working today moving Joe's sheep, so he couldn't come for a visit. Has your father found work?"

"Yes, I mean, *ja,* at the sawmill. Mrs. Weaver is glad, too, because that silly boy Faron Martin couldn't keep his mind off his girlfriend long enough to do his work."

Carl heard a smothered chuckle from Lizzie. He had to smile, too. "I'm not sure your grandmother and Mrs. Weaver want you repeating their conversations."

"Why not?"

The two boys reached her before Carl could explain. The oldest boy, Jacob Imhoff, spoke first. "Joy, you aren't supposed to run off without telling someone. You know that."

She hung her head. "I forgot."

Joy had a bad habit of wandering off and had frightened her family on several occasions by disappearing without letting anyone know where she was going.

The younger boy, her cousin David, took her hand. "That's okay. We aren't mad."

She peeked at him. "You're not?"

"Nee."

She gave him a sheepish smile. "I only wanted to talk to Carl."

A car buzzed past them on the highway. Jacob patted her shoulder. "We don't want you to get hit by one of the *Englisch* cars driving by so fast."

"This was my fault," Carl said quickly. "I should have turned into the lane to speak to Joy and not stopped out here on the road."

Joy stared at him solemnly. "It's okay. I forgive you."

If only he could gain forgiveness so easily for his past sins. He quickly changed the subject. "How is your puppy, Joy?"

"Pickles is a butterball with legs and a tail. She chews up everything. Mammi is getting mighty tired of it."

Joy could always make him smile. "Tell your grandmother to give your pup a soupbone to gnaw on. That will keep her sharp little teeth occupied for a few days."

Joy looked past him at Lizzie. "Is this your wife? She's pretty."

He sat bolt upright. *"Nee, sie ist nicht meine frau.* She's not my wife."

Lizzie watched a blush burn a fiery red path up Carl's neck and engulf his face. It was amusing to see such a big man discomforted by a child's innocent question, but she was more interested in his answer. He had denied that she was his wife in flawless Pennsylvania Dutch, the German dialect language spoken by the Amish.

Carl King might dress and act Englisch, but he had surely been raised Amish to speak the language so well.

He gathered the reins. "You should get back to your game, kids. I have to take this lady to the bus station."

He set the pony moving again, and a frown replaced the smile he had given so easily to the little girl. Lizzie liked him better when he was smiling.

"Your Pennsylvania Dutch is very good."

"I get by."

"Were you raised Amish?"

A muscle twitched in his clenched jaw. "I was."

"Several of the young men in our community have left before they were baptized, too."

"I left afterward."

Lizzie's eyes widened with shock. That meant he was in the Bann. Why had her grandfather allowed her to travel with him? Her uncle wouldn't even speak with an excommunicated person. A second later, she realized that she would very likely be placed in the Bann, too. Her uncle would not let her rebellious action go unpunished. She prayed her sisters were not suffering because of her.

She glanced at Carl and noted the tense set of his jaw. The rules of her faith were clear. She could not accept a ride from a shunned person. She was forbidden to do business with him, accept any favor from him or eat at the same table. Her grandfather had placed her in a very awkward situation. "Please stop the cart."

Carl's shoulders slumped. "As you wish."

He pulled the pony to a halt. "It is a long walk. You will miss the bus."

"Then I must drive. It is permitted for me to give you a lift, but I can't accept one from you."

"I know the rules." He laid down the reins and stepped over the bench seat to sit on the floor of the cart behind her.

She took the reins and slapped them against the pony's rump to get him moving. He broke into a brisk trot.

"How is it that you work for my grandfather? Has he left the church, too?"

"No."

"Does he know your circumstance?"

"Of course."

She grew more confused by the minute. "Surely the members of his congregation must object to his continued association with you."

"He hasn't mentioned it if they do."

She glanced toward him over her shoulder. "But they know, don't they?"

"You'd have to ask Joe about that."

As she was on her way to the bus depot, that wasn't likely to happen. "I would, but I doubt I'll see him again." She heard the bitterness in her voice and knew Carl heard it, too.

Her grandfather had made it crystal clear he wasn't interested in getting to know his granddaughters. His rejection hurt deeply, but she shouldn't have been surprised by it. To depend on any man's kindness was asking for heartache.

As the pony trotted along, Lizzie struggled to find forgiveness in her heart. Her grandfather was a man who needed prayers, not her harsh thoughts. She prayed for Carl, too, that he would repent his sins, whatever they were, and find his way back to God. His life must be lonely indeed.

As lonely as Clara's would be married to a man she

didn't love and without her sisters around her. Lizzie had failed her miserably.

After they had traveled nearly a mile, Lizzie decided she didn't care to spend the rest of the trip in silence. It left her too much time to think about her failure. Conversation with a shunned person wasn't strictly forbidden. "Is Joy a relative?"

"A neighbor."

"She seems like a very sweet child."

"Yes."

"Who is Duncan?"

"My dog."

His curt answers made her think he'd left his good humor back at the schoolyard. She gave up the idea of maintaining a conversation. She drew a deep breath and tried to come up with a new course of action that would save her sisters.

All she could think of was to find a job in town, but she didn't have enough money to rent a room. She had enough to pay for her bus fare home and that was it. She didn't even have enough left over to buy something to eat. Her stomach grumbled in protest. She hadn't eaten in more than a day. Nothing since her last supper at her uncle's house.

If she returned to his home, she would have to beg forgiveness and endure his chastisement in whatever form he chose. It would most likely be a whipping with his favorite willow cane, but he sometimes chose a leather strap. Stale bread and water for a week was another punishment he enjoyed handing out. She would be blessed if that were his choice. She shivered and pulled her coat tight across her chest.

"Are you cold?" Carl asked.

"A little." More than a little, she realized. There was

a bite to the wind now that they were heading into it. A stubborn March was holding spring at bay.

Carl slipped off his coat and laid it on the seat. "Put this on."

She shook her head. "I can't take your coat."

"You are cold. I'm not."

She glanced back at him sitting braced against the side of the cart. "*Nee,* it wouldn't be right."

He studied her for a few seconds, then looked away. A dull flush of red stained his cheeks. "It is permitted if you do not take it from my hand."

"That's not what I meant. I don't wish to cause you discomfort."

"Watching you shiver causes me discomfort."

It was hard to argue with that logic. She picked up the thick coat and slipped it on. It retained his body heat and felt blissfully warm as she pulled it close. *"Danki."*

"You're welcome."

They rode in silence for the rest of the way into town. As they drove past the local inn, she turned to him. "I wish to stop here for a few minutes. Since my grandfather won't help us, I must try to find a job."

"He told me to take you to the bus station."

"I'll only be a few minutes."

He grudgingly nodded. "A few minutes and then we must go. I have work to do."

"Danki." She gave him a bright smile before she unwrapped herself from his coat and jumped down from the cart.

When she entered the inn, she found herself inside a lobby with ceilings that rose two stories above her. On one side of the room, glass shelves displayed an assortment of jams and jellies for sale. On the opposite wall, an impressive stone fireplace soared two stories high and was at least eight feet wide. Made in the old-world fashion using rounded river stones set in mortar, it boasted a massive timber for a mantel. A quilt hanger had been added near the top. A beautiful star quilt hung on display. Two more quilts folded over racks flanked the fireplace.

At the far end of the room was a waist-high counter. A matronly Amish woman stood behind it. Tall and big-boned with gray hair beneath her white *kapp,* she wore a soft blue dress that matched her eyes. "Good afternoon and *willkommen* to the Wadler Inn. I'm Naomi Wadler. How may I help you?"

Her friendly smile immediately put Lizzie at ease. "I'm looking for work. Anything will do. I'm not picky."

"I'm sorry. We don't have any openings right now. Are you new to the area? You look familiar. Have we met?"

Lizzie tried to hide her disappointment at not finding employment. "I don't think so. Might you know of someone looking for a chore girl or household helper?"

"I don't, dear. If I hear of anything, I'll be glad to let you know. Where are you staying?"

Lizzie glanced out the window. Carl was scowling in her direction. He motioned for her to come on. She turned back to Naomi. "That's okay. I thank you for your time. The quilts around the fireplace are lovely. Are they your work?"

"*Nee,* I display them for some of our local quilters. Many Englisch guests come to this area looking to buy quilts. These were done by a local woman named Rebecca Troyer. I'm always looking for quilts to buy if you have some to sell."

All she had was her mother's quilt, and it was too precious to part with. "My sister has a good hand with a needle. I'm afraid I don't, but I can cook, clean, tend a garden, milk cows. I can even help with little children."

Naomi gave her a sympathetic smile. "You should check over at the newspaper office, *Miller Press*. It's a few blocks from here. They may know of someone looking for work."

Lizzie started for the door. As she reached it, the woman called out, "I didn't get your name, child."

"I'm Lizzie Barkman. I have to go. Thank you again for your time." She left the inn and climbed into the cart again. "They don't have anything. I wish to stop at the newspaper office. There might be something in the help-wanted section of the paper."

"Joe can't move all the sheep without help. I should be there."

"It will only take a minute or two to read the want ads. I'll hurry, I promise. Which way is it?"

He gave her directions and she found the *Miller Press* office without difficulty. Inside, she quickly read through the ads, but didn't find anything she thought she could do. Most of them were requests for skilled labor. It looked as if going home was to be her fate, after all.

With lagging steps, she returned to the cart. She followed Carl's succinct directions to the center of town. When the bus station came into view, she felt the sting of tears again. She'd arrived that morning, tired but full of hope, certain that she could save her sister.

It had been a foolhardy plan at best. She stared at the building. "My sister was right. I'm nothing but a dreamer."

A short, bald man came out the door and locked it behind him. Carl took Lizzie's suitcase from the back of the cart and approached him. "This lady needs a ticket."

"Sorry, we're closed." The man didn't even look up. He started to walk off, but Carl blocked his way.

"She needs a ticket to Indiana."

The stationmaster took a step back. "You're too late.

The westbound bus left five minutes ago. The next one is on Tuesday."

"Four days? How can that be?"

The little man raised his hands. "Look around. We're not exactly a transportation hub. Hope Springs is just down the road from Next-to-Nowhere. The bus going west departs at 3:00 p.m. on Tuesdays and Fridays." He stepped around Carl and walked away.

She wasn't going back today. She still had a chance to find a job. Lizzie looked skyward and breathed a quick prayer. "*Danki,* my Lord."

She wanted to shout for joy, but the grim look on Carl's face kept her silent. He scowled at her. "Joe isn't going to like this."

Chapter Three

"What is she doing back here? I told you to make sure she got on the bus!" Joe looked ready to spit nails.

Carl jumped down from the back of the cart and took Lizzie's suitcase and her box from behind the seat. He knew Joe would be upset. He wasn't looking forward to this conversation.

"She missed the bus. The next one going her way is on Tuesday. I couldn't very well leave her standing on the street corner, could I?"

"I don't see why not," Joe grumbled.

Lizzie got down for the cart and came up the steps to stand by her grandfather on the porch. "I'm sorry to inconvenience you, Daadi, but I didn't know what else to do. I don't have enough money to pay for a room at the inn until Tuesday and get a ticket home. I won't be any trouble."

"Too late for that," Carl muttered. She had already cost him half a day's work.

"What am I supposed to do with you now?" Joe demanded.

"I can sleep in the barn if you don't have room for me in the house."

She actually looked demure with her hands clasped before her and her eyes downcast. Carl wasn't fooled. She was tickled pink that she had missed the bus. He half wondered if she had insisted on making those job-hunting stops for just that reason. He had no proof of that, but he wasn't sure he would put it past her.

Joe sighed heavily. "I guess you can stay in your mother's old bedroom upstairs, but don't expect there to be clean sheets on the bed."

Lizzie smiled sweetly. "*Danki.* I'm not afraid of a little dust. If you really want me to leave, you could hire a driver to take me home."

Scowling, Joe snapped, "I'm not paying a hired driver to take you back. It would cost a fortune. You will leave on Tuesday. Since you're here, you might as well cook supper. You can cook, can't you?"

"Of course."

He gestured toward the door. "Come on, Carl. Those shearing pens won't set themselves up."

She shot Carl a sharp look and then leaned toward Joe. "Daadi, may I speak to you in private?"

Here it comes. She's going to pressure Joe to get rid of me.

Carl didn't want to leave. He enjoyed working with the sheep and with Joe. In this place, he had found a small measure of peace that didn't seem to exist anywhere else in the world. Would Lizzie make trouble for the old man if he allowed Carl to stay on?

Joe waved aside her request. "We'll speak after supper. My work can't wait any longer. Carl, did you pick up the mail, at least?"

He shook his head. "I forgot to mention it when we passed your mailbox."

Joe glared at Lizzie. "That's what comes of having a distraction around. I'll go myself."

"I'll go get your mail." Lizzie started to climb back onto the cart, but Joe stopped her.

"The pony has done enough work today. It won't hurt you to walk to the end of the lane, will it?"

She flushed and stepped away from the cart. "*Nee,* of course not. Shall I unhitch him and put him away?"

"Put him in the corral to the right of the barn and make sure you rub him down good."

"I will."

As she led the pony away, sympathy for her stirred in Carl. Joe wasn't usually so unkind. "I can take care of the horse, Joe."

"If she's going to stay, she's going to earn her keep while she's here. I don't know why she had to come in the first place." Joe stalked away with a deep frown on his face.

Carl followed him. The two men crossed to the largest shed and went inside. Numerous metal panels were stacked against the far wall. They were used to make pens of various sizes to hold the sheep both prior to shearing and afterward.

They had the first three pens assembled before Joe spoke again. "You think I'm being too hard on her, don't you?"

"It's your business and none of mine."

"What did she have to say on your trip into town and back?"

"Not much. She's concerned that her sister is being made to marry against her will by their uncle Morris. It's not the way things are done around here."

"*Nee,* but it doesn't surprise me much. I never cared for Morris. I couldn't believe it when my daughter wanted to marry into that family. I tried to talk her out of it. I've never met a more shiftless lot. The men never worked harder than they had to, but they made sure the women did. In my eyes, they didn't treat their women with the respect they deserved."

"What do you mean?"

"They spoke harshly to them. They kept them away from other women. I saw fear in the eyes of Morris's wife more than once when he got upset with her."

"Do you believe there was physical abuse?"

"I thought so, but none of them would admit it. Such things weren't talked about back then. I went so far as to share my misgivings with the bishop. The family didn't take kindly to my interference."

"I imagine not."

"My daughter assured me her husband was a kind man, but I saw the signs. I saw the changes in her over the years. My son-in-law and I had some heated words about it. Then one day, the whole family up and moved away. I never saw them again. My daughter never even wrote to let me know where they had gone. Years later, I got one letter. It was from Morris telling me my Abigail and her husband were dead. He said a truck struck their buggy. Her husband died instantly, but Abigail lingered for another day."

Joe's voice tapered off as he struggled with his emotions. Carl had never seen him so upset. After giving the old man a few minutes to compose himself, Carl said, "I've never heard of the Amish having arranged marriages."

"They don't, but if you dig deep enough in any barrel, you'll find a few bad apples, even among the Amish. Morris was a bad apple. I don't know why my girl couldn't see that, but I was told she lived long enough after the accident to name Morris as guardian of her children. I'm not surprised he thinks he can pick their husbands."

"So, you aren't going to help Lizzie?"

Joe shook his head slowly. "I loved my daughter, Carl. I never got over her leaving the way she did, but she was a good mother. I have to ask myself what would she want me to do. Honestly, I think my daughter would want me to stay out of it. Life is not easy for any of us. I don't want Lizzie to think she can come running to me whenever it seems too hard for her."

"Do you really think that's what she's doing?" Carl asked gently.

"I don't know. Maybe."

Carl didn't agree, but then it wasn't his place to agree or disagree with Joe. It was his place to take care of the sheep.

"What else did she say?" Joe asked. He tried to sound indifferent, but Carl wasn't fooled.

"She wants to find a job around here."

Joe nodded but didn't comment. Carl drew a deep breath. "I had to tell her I'm in the Bann."

"*Ach,* that's none of her business." Joe kicked a stubborn panel into place and secured it with a length of wire.

"She asked. I couldn't lie."

Joe shared a rare, stilted smile. "It would astonish me if you did."

"Will she go to church services with you on Sunday?"

"*Ja,* I imagine so."

"Will my being here cause trouble for you?" He didn't want to leave, but he would. Joe had been good to him.

"Having her here is causing me trouble."

"You know what I mean." Joe could easily find himself shunned by his fellow church members for allowing Carl to work on his farm. The rules were clear about what was permitted and what wasn't with a shunned person. Joe had been bending the rules for more than two years to give Carl a place to live. A few people in Joe's church might suspect Carl was ex-Amish, but no one knew it for a fact. Only Lizzie. If she spread that information, it would change everything.

The old man sighed and laid a hand on Carl's shoulder. "*Sohn,* I know I'm not a good example. I don't like most people, but that's my fault and not theirs. Folks around here are generous and accepting of others. I've known Bishop Zook since he was a toddler. He's a kind and just man. I don't know your story, Carl, but I've come to know you. You seek solitude out among the flocks and in your small hut, but it does not bring you peace. 'Tis plain you carry a heavy burden. If you repent, if you ask forgiveness, it will be granted."

Carl looked away from the sympathy he didn't deserve. "Sometimes, forgiveness must be earned."

Joe's grip on Carl's shoulder tightened. "Our Lord Jesus earned it for us all by his death on the cross. However, it's your life. Live as you must. I've never pried and I never will."

"Thanks, but you didn't answer my question. Will my staying here cause trouble for you?"

Joe dusted his hands together. "I can handle any trouble my granddaughter tries to make."

Carl wasn't as confident.

The evening shadows were growing long by the time they finished setting up the runways and pens. Both men were tired, hot and sweaty, in spite of the cold weather. Carl found he was eager to see how Lizzie was faring. Was she a good cook? Joe wasn't. Carl managed, but he didn't enjoy the task.

The two men entered the kitchen and stopped in their tracks. They both looked around in surprise. The clutter had been cleared from the table. The wild heaps of dishes and pans in the sink had been tamed, washed and put away. The blue-and-white-checkered plastic tablecloth was glistening wet, as if she had just finished wiping it down. Even the floor had been swept and mopped. The scuffed old black-and-white linoleum looked better than Carl had ever seen it. There was a lingering scent of pine cleaner in the air, but it was the smell of simmering stew that made his mouth water.

Lizzie stood at the stove with her back to them. "It's almost done. There's soap and a fresh towel at the sink for you."

She turned toward them and used her forearm to sweep back a few locks of bright red hair that had escaped from beneath her black *kapp*. Her cheeks were flushed from the heat of the oven. Carl was struck once again by how pretty she was and how natural she looked in Joe's kitchen.

If the aroma was anything to go by, this might be the best meal he'd had in months. His stomach growled in anticipation, but he didn't move. The arrangement he and Joe shared might be different now that Lizzie was with them. He locked eyes with Joe and waited for a sign from him.

Lizzie wasn't sure how to proceed. She'd never fixed a meal for a shunned person. If Carl sat at the table, she would have to eat standing at the counter or in the other room. Eating at the same table with someone in the Bann was forbidden. Had her grandfather been breaking the Ordnung by eating with Carl? If so, it was her solemn duty to inform his bishop of such an infraction. She quailed at the thought. Such a move on her part would ruin any chance of bringing her sisters to live with him.

She watched as her grandfather went to the sink beneath the window and washed the grime off his hands. He used the towel she'd placed there and left it lying on the counter so that Carl could use it, too.

Her *daadi* stepped to the table, moved aside one of the benches and flipped back the tablecloth. Puzzled, Lizzie wondered what he was doing. Then she saw it wasn't one large kitchen table. It was two smaller ones that had been pushed together. He pulled the tables a few inches apart, smoothed the cloth back into place and returned the bench to its original place.

She relaxed with relief. Her grandfather hadn't broken the Ordnung. It appeared that he and Carl maintained the separation dictated by the Amish faith even when no one was around.

She caught Carl's quick glance before he looked away. He said, "Is this arrangement suitable, or should I eat outside?"

He was trying to look as if it didn't matter, but she could tell that it did.

"If my grandfather feels this is acceptable, then it is." It was his home, and he had to follow the rules of his congregation. It wouldn't have been acceptable in her uncle's home. Her uncle wouldn't have allowed Carl inside the house. Her uncle expounded often about the dangers of associating with unclean people.

Joe took his place at the head of the table. Lizzie dished stew into a bowl and placed it in front of him. She dished up a second bowl and gave Carl a sympathetic look before she left it on the counter. She took a plate of golden-brown biscuits from the oven and set it on the table, too.

Carl washed up and carried his bowl to his table opposite her grandfather.

Lizzie got her own bowl and took a seat at her grandfather's left-hand side. When she was settled, he bowed his head and silently gave thanks to God for the meal. From the corner of her eye, she saw Carl bow his head, too.

What had he done that made him an outsider among them, and why was her grandfather risking being shunned himself by having him around?

The meal progressed in silence. Lizzie didn't mind; it

was normal at her uncle's home, too. She and her sisters saved their conversations until they were getting ready for bed at night.

The unexpected weight of loneliness forced her spirits lower. She missed her sisters more than she thought possible. Tonight, she would be alone for the first time in her life. She didn't count her night on the bus, for she hadn't been alone for a minute on that horrible ride. She thought she was hungry, but her appetite ebbed away. She picked at her food and pushed it around in her bowl. A quick glance at her grandfather and Carl showed neither of them noticed. They ate with gusto. Maybe good food would convince them they needed a woman around the house full-time.

A woman, yes, but four women?

There was more than enough work to keep four women busy for months. The place was a mess. All the rooms needed a thorough cleaning. There was years of accumulated dust and cobwebs in every corner of the four bedrooms upstairs, although only one room contained a bed. The others held an accumulation of odds and ends, broken furniture and several plastic tubs filled with baby bottles. She assumed they were for the lambs.

The downstairs wasn't as bad, but it wasn't tidy, either. She was afraid to speculate on the amount of mending that was needed. There was a pile of clothes in a huge laundry hamper beside the wringer washer on a small back porch. The few bits of clothing she had examined were both dirty and in need of repair. It was too bad that one of her days here was a Sunday. She wouldn't be able to engage in anything but the most necessary work on the Sabbath.

She'd simply have to rise early tomorrow and again on Monday and Tuesday mornings to get as much of the washing, mending and cleaning done as she could before her bus left. Her grandfather might not want her here, but she would do all that she could for him before she left, even if she disliked mending with a passion.

It was a shame that Clara hadn't come with her. Clara loved needlework. Her tiny stitches were much neater than Lizzie could manage. Each of the girls had a special talent. Lizzie liked to cook. Betsy was good with animals. Clara, like their mother, enjoyed sewing, quilting and knitting. Greta avoided housework whenever she could. She enjoyed being outside tending the orchard and the gardens.

Just thinking about them made a deep sadness settle in Lizzie's soul. She had failed miserably to help them thus far, but the good Lord had given her more time. She wouldn't waste it feeling sorry for herself.

She smiled at her grandfather. "I hope you like the stew. I do enjoy cooking. I couldn't help noticing your garden hasn't been prepared for spring planting yet. It's nearly time to get peas and potatoes planted. My sister Greta would be itching to spade up the dirt. The Lord blessed her with a green thumb for sure."

Her grandfather ran his last bite of biscuit around the rim of his bowl to sop up any traces of gravy. "The planting will get done after the lambing."

"Of course. You probably know there's barely any preserved food left in the cellar. I used the last of the canned beef and carrots for tonight's meal. There will be only canned chicken for the next meals unless you can provide me with something fresh or allow me to go into town and purchase more food. What a shame it is to see an Amish cellar bare. At home, my sisters and I have hundreds of jars of meat, corn and vegetables. Do you like beets, Daadi?"

"Not particularly."

"I like snap peas better myself." She fell silent.

"There are plenty of eggs in the henhouse. We men know how to make do."

There had to be a way to convince him of her usefulness. Perhaps after he saw the results of her hard work over the next several days he would agree to let her stay.

Joe pushed his empty bowl away and brushed biscuit crumbs from his beard and vest. "You're a *goot* cook, I'll give you that."

"A mighty good cook. Thank you for the meal," Carl added.

"You're welcome." She wasn't used to being thanked for doing something that was her normal responsibility.

Her grandfather swallowed the last swig of his coffee and set the cup in his bowl. "I reckon it's time to start moving the flocks closer to the barns."

Carl nodded. "I can put the rams and the first of the ewes in the barn tomorrow in separate pens."

"No point penning them inside just yet. Monday will be soon enough. Shearing can start on Tuesday."

Lizzie brightened. Perhaps the sheep held the key to proving her usefulness. "Can I help with that? I'd love to learn more about sheep and about shearing them."

Joe huffed in disgust. "If you don't know sheep, you'll be no use to me."

She looked at Carl. He didn't say anything. She was foolish to hope for help in that direction. Suddenly, she remembered the mail she had collected earlier. There had been a letter for him. She went into the living room and returned with her grandfather's copy of the local newspaper and an envelope for Carl.

Her grandfather's eyes brighten. "*Ach,* my newspaper. *Danki.* I like reading it after supper."

She turned to Carl and held the letter toward him. "This came for you."

When he didn't take it, she laid it on the corner of the table and resumed her seat.

Rising to his feet, Carl picked up the letter, glanced at it and then carried his empty bowl to the sink. Turning to the stove, he lifted the lid on the firebox and dropped the letter in unopened. He left the house without another word.

After the screen door banged shut behind him, Lizzie gathered the rest of the dishes and carried them to the sink. She stared out the window at his retreating back as he walked toward the barn and the pasture gate beyond.

His dog came bounding across the yard and danced around him, seeking attention. He paused long enough to bend and pat the animal. Straightening, he glanced back once at the house before he walked on.

What had he done to cut himself off from his family, his friends and from his Amish faith? Why burn an unopened letter? Why live such a lonely life with only a dog and an old man for company? Carl King was an intriguing man. The longer she was around him, the more she wanted to uncover the answers about him.

"Out with your questions before you choke on them," her grandfather said, still seated at the table.

"I don't know what you mean." She began filling the sink with water.

"*Ja,* you do. You want to know about Carl."

She couldn't very well deny it when she was bursting with curiosity about the man. She shut off the water and faced her grandfather. "I don't understand how you can do business with him. It is forbidden."

"I do no business with him." He opened his paper and began to read.

She took a step toward him in disbelief and propped both hands on her hips. "How can you say that? He works for you. He's your hired man."

"I did not hire Carl. He works here because he wishes

to do so. He lives in an empty hut on my property. He pays no rent, so I am neither landlord nor employer."

"You mean he works for nothing?"

Folding his paper in exasperation, he said, "Each year, when the lambs are sold, I leave one third of my profits here on the kitchen table, and I go to bed. In the morning, the money is always gone."

"So you do pay him?"

"I have never asked if he's the one who takes the money."

She crossed her arms over her chest. "Don't you think that is splitting hairs?"

"No doubt some people will say it is."

"Aren't you worried that you may be shunned for his continued presence here?"

He leaned back in his chair. "What would you have me do?"

"You must tell him that unless he repents, he must leave. What has he done to make all your church avoid him?"

"I have no idea."

"But all members of the church must agree to the shunning. How can you not know the reason? It is not a thing that is done lightly or in secret."

"In all my years, I have seen it done only a handful of times. It was very sad and distressful for those involved. Carl is not from around here. He has not been shunned by my congregation. I would not have known he was anything but an Englisch fellow in need of a meal and a bed if he hadn't told me. It seems to me that he holds our beliefs in high regard."

"Then for him to remain separated from the church is doubly wrong, and all the more reason to send him away."

Her grandfather let his chair down and leaned forward

with his hands clasped on the table. "Child, why do we shun someone?"

"Because they have broken their vows to God and to the church by refusing to follow the Ordnung."

"You have missed the meaning of my question. What is the purpose of shunning an individual?"

"To make them see the error of their ways."

"That is true, but you have not mentioned the most important part. It is not to punish them. Shunning is done out of love for that person so that they may see what it is to be cut off from God and God's family by their sin. It is a difficult thing to do, to care for someone and yet turn away from them."

"But if they don't repent, we must turn away so that we do not share in that sin."

"If I give aid to a sinner, does that make me one?"

"Of course not. We are commanded to care for those in need, be they family or stranger."

"As the Good Samaritan did in the parable told by our Lord."

She could see where his questions were leading. "*Ja,* if you have given aid to Carl, that is as it should be."

A smile twitched at the corner of his mouth. "I'm glad you approve. The first time I met Carl, I discovered him sleeping in my barn. It had rained like mad in the night. His clothes were ragged and damp. They hung on his thin frame like a scarecrow's outfit. Everything he owned in the world he was wearing or had rolled up in a pack he was using as a pillow, except for a skinny puppy that lay beside him.

"Carl immediately got up, apologized for trespassing and said he was leaving. I offered him a meal. He declined, but said he would be grateful if I could spare something for the dog."

Lizzie's heart twisted with pity for Carl. To be homeless and alone was no easy thing. "I assume you fed the dog?"

"I told Carl I had a little bacon I could fry up for the pup. I coaxed them both into the house and fried enough for all of us. I put a plate on the floor and that little Duncan gobbled it up before I got my hand out of the way. Bacon is still his favorite food. When I put two plates on the table was when Carl told me he could not eat with me."

"At least he was honest about it."

"If you had seen the look in that young man's eyes, you would know, as I do, that he cares deeply about our faith. He was starving, but he was willing to forgo food in order to keep me from unknowingly breaking the laws of our church."

"Yet, he never told you why he had been placed in the Bann?"

"*Nee,* he has not, and I do not ask. I told him I had an empty hut he could use for as long as he wanted. His dog took naturally to working the sheep and so did Carl. He has a tender heart for animals."

"What you did was a great kindness, Daadi, but Carl no longer requires physical aid."

"True. The man is neither hungry nor homeless, but his great wound is not yet healed. That's why I have not turned him away."

She scowled. "I saw no evidence of an injury."

Her grandfather shook his head sadly. "Then you have not looked into his eyes as I have done. Carl has a grave wound inside. Something in his past lies heavy on his mind and on his heart. My instincts tell me he will find his way back to God and to our faith when he has had time to heal. Then there will be great rejoicing in heaven and on earth."

Maybe she came by her daydreaming naturally, after all. "*If* it happens."

Her grandfather sighed, rose from his chair and headed toward his bedroom. Before he closed the door, he turned back to her. "It will happen. It's a shame you won't be here to see it when it does."

Chapter Four

He wouldn't go up to the house today.

Carl stood in the doorway of his one-room hut and stared at the smoke rising from Joe's chimney a quarter of a mile away. The chimney was all he could see of the house, for the barn sat between it and his abode.

It hadn't taken Carl long to decide that avoiding Lizzie would be his best course of action. It was clear how uncomfortable his presence made her last night. He didn't want her to endure more of the same.

Her presence made him uncomfortable, too.

She made him think about all he had lost the right to know. A home, a wife, the simple pleasure of sitting at a table with someone.

No, he wouldn't go up to the house, but he knew she was there.

Was she making breakfast? If it was half as good as supper had been, it would be delicious. He couldn't remember the last time he'd had such light and fluffy biscuits.

Even for another biscuit, he wouldn't go up the hill.

He could make do with a slice of stale bread and cheese from his own tiny kitchen. He didn't need biscuits. He didn't even need coffee.

And he sure didn't need to see her again.

Lizzie Barkman's pretty face was etched in his mind like a carving in stone. All he had to do was close his eyes, and he could see her as clearly as if she were standing in front of him.

He hadn't slept well, but when he dozed, it was her face he saw in his dreams and not the usual faces from his nightmares.

In his dream last night, Lizzie had been smiling at him, beckoning him from a doorway to come inside a warm, snug house. He wanted to go in, but his feet had been frozen to the ground as snow swirled around him. Sometimes, the snow grew so thick it hid her face, but as soon as it cleared a little, she was still there waiting for him—a wonderful, warm vision in a cold, lonely world.

Carl shook his head to dispel the memory. No, he wouldn't go up to the house today. She wouldn't beckon him inside, and he shouldn't go in if she did. He was a forbidden one, an outcast by his own making.

He needed to stop feeling sorry for himself. He had work to do. He glanced toward the sturdy doghouse just outside his doorway. "Come on, Duncan. We have sheep to move today."

Duncan didn't appear. Carl leaned down to look inside and saw the doghouse was empty. Puzzled, he glanced around the pasture. His dog was nowhere in sight. Carl cupped his hands around his mouth and hollered the dog's name. Duncan still didn't come.

This wasn't like him. The only time the dog occasionally roamed away from the farm was when school was in session. He liked to play fetch with the kids and visit with the teacher's pretty female shepherd. It was too early for the children or the teacher to be at school yet, so where was Duncan?

Maybe Joe had taken him and gone out after some of the sheep already. If that was the case, Carl had better see that the fences in the hilltop enclosure around the lambing sheds were in good repair.

He headed up to the barn and found Joe pitching hay down to the horses in the corral. If he hadn't gone after the sheep, where was the dog? "Joe, have you seen Duncan this morning?"

Joe paused and leaned on his pitchfork handle. "*Nee,* I have not. He's not with you?"

Carl shook his head. "He was gone when I got up."

"He'll be back. Lizzie should have breakfast ready in a few minutes. Tell her I'll be in when I'm done here." Joe resumed his work.

"I'm not hungry. I'm going to fix the fence in the little field at the top of the hill, and then I'll move the ewes in the south forty up to it. They'll be easier to move into the barn from there when it's time to shear them."

"All right."

Carl knew if he took two steps to the left, he'd have a good view of the house from around the corner of the barn. "It'll make it easier to keep an eye on them for any early lambs, too."

"It will." Joe kept pitching down forkfuls of hay.

"I don't expect any premature births from that group. They've all had lambs before without any trouble."

"I know."

Carl folded his arms tight across his chest and tried to ignore the overpowering urge to look and see if he could catch a glimpse of Lizzie. "We might have to cull a few of them. We've got five or six that are getting up there in years."

Joe stopped his work and leaned on his pitchfork again.

"I'm not senile yet. I know my own sheep. I thought you were looking for your dog."

"I was. I am."

"Have you checked up at the house?"

"No." Carl unfolded his arms and slipped his hands into his front pockets.

"That granddaughter of mine was singing this morning. Could be the dog thought it was yowling, and he's gone to investigate."

"Is she a poor singer?" Somehow, Carl expected her to have a melodious voice to match her sweet smile.

"How do I know? I've been tone-deaf since I was born. It all sounds like yowling to me." Setting his pitchfork aside, Joe vanished into the recesses of the hayloft.

Now that he was unobserved, Carl took those two steps and glanced toward the house. He didn't see Lizzie, but Duncan sat just outside the screen door, intently watching something inside.

"Duncan. Here, boy!"

The dog glanced his way and went back to staring into the house. He barked once. Annoyed, Carl began walking toward him. "Duncan, get your sorry tail over here. We've got work to do."

The dog rose to his feet, but didn't leave his place.

Carl approached the house just as the screen door opened a crack. The dog wagged his tail vigorously. Carl saw Lizzie bend down and slip Duncan something to eat.

After deciding he wouldn't see her at all today, that tiny glimpse of her wasn't enough. He wanted to look upon her face again. Would she welcome his company or simply tolerate it?

It didn't matter. He had no business thinking it might. What had Joe told her about him last night? Carl kept walking in spite of his better judgment telling him to go gather the flock without his dog.

By the time he reached the door, Lizzie had gone back inside, but the smell of frying bacon lingered in the air.

Carl stared down at his dog. "I see she's discovered your weakness."

Duncan licked his chops.

Carl grinned. "*Ja,* I've got a strong liking for bacon myself."

"Come in and have a seat before these eggs get cold. I hope you like them scrambled." Her cheerful voice drove away the last of his hesitation. She was going to be here for only a few days. Why shouldn't he enjoy her company and her cooking until she left?

He moved Duncan aside with his knee and pulled open the screen door. The dog followed him in and took his usual place beneath the bench Carl sat on. Duncan knew better than to beg for food, but he would happily snatch up any bits his master slipped to him. It was a morning ritual that had gone on for years.

The house smelled of bacon and fresh-baked bread. Lizzie must have been up for hours. She stood at the stove stirring something. There were two plates piled high with food already on the counter. Carl sat down and waited. "Joe will be in shortly."

She took her pan from the stove and poured creamy gravy into a serving boat on the counter beside her. "*Goot.* I ate earlier. I have a load of clothes in the washer I need to hang out. Having a propane-powered washer is so nice. At home, we do all the laundry by hand." Turning around, her eyes widened with shock. "No! Out, out, out!"

Carl leaped up from his seat. "I'm sorry. I thought it was all right if I ate here."

"You, yes. The dog, no."

It took him a second to process what she meant. "But Duncan normally eats with me at breakfast."

She plunked the gravy boat on the table. "Then he will be thrilled when I'm gone. But until I leave this house, I won't tolerate a dog in my kitchen at mealtime. Look what his muddy feet have done to my clean floor. Take him outside." She crossed her arms over her chest and glared at them both.

So much for basking in the glow of her smile this morning. Carl looked down and saw she was right. Muddy paw prints stood out in sharp contrast to the clean black-and-white squares. The dog must have gone down to the creek before coming to the house.

Duncan sank as flat against the floor as he could get. He knew he was in trouble, but Carl was sure he didn't understand why.

"Come on, fella. Outside with you."

Duncan didn't move.

Carl took hold of his collar and had to pull him out from under the table. His muddy feet left a long smear until Duncan realized he wasn't welcome. Then he bolted for the door and shot outside as Joe came, in nearly tripping the old gent.

"What's the matter with him?"

"His feet are muddy," Carl said. He left the kitchen and went out to the back porch. He returned with a mop and bucket. He started to wipe up the mess.

Already seated at the table, Joe said, "Leave the woman's work to the woman."

"It was my dog that made the mess." Carl met Lizzie's eyes. They were wide with surprise. Suddenly, she smiled at him. It was worth a week of mopping floors to behold. He leaned on the mop handle and smiled back.

* * *

Lizzie realized Carl's bold gaze was fixed on her. And why shouldn't it be? She wasn't behaving in the least like a modest maiden. She averted her eyes and schooled her features into what she hoped was a prim attitude. It was hard when his presence made her heart race. He was a handsome fellow, but she shouldn't be staring at him.

"Am I getting breakfast, or should I go out and get the rest of my work done?" Joe snapped.

"I'm sorry, Daadi. I have it right here." She hurried to bring both plates to the table. Keeping her eyes downcast, she said, "I'll take the mop out to the porch. I'm going that way. It was kind of you to help."

"It's no trouble. I'll take it out."

"As you wish." She scurried ahead of him out the back door and stopped when she had the tub of the wringer washer between them.

He emptied the pail out the back door and placed it with the mop in the corner. When he didn't go back inside the house, she realized he wanted to say more.

"Is there something else?" *Please let it be quick and then please let him go away.* He made her nervous, but in a strange edgy way that she didn't understand.

"I know you hope your grandfather will let you and your sisters live here. I can see you're trying to please him. I don't think Joe will change his mind, but there are a few things you should know about him."

"Such as?"

"He mentioned you were singing this morning."

So her grandfather had noticed. She brightened. "I was. Did he like it?"

"Joe is tone-deaf. Singing is just noise to him."

"Oh." That was a letdown. She hoped a happy attitude and a cheerful hymn would soften his heart.

"And there is something else," Carl said.

She crossed her arms. "What?"

"Don't jump to do his bidding. He doesn't like people who are spineless."

Indignation flared in her. "Are you saying I'm spineless?"

"No, not at all. It took courage to come here. Just stand your ground and don't pander to him."

She relaxed when she realized he was honestly trying to help. "I appreciate your advice. I imagine you think I'm being underhanded by seeking to worm my way into his affections."

"No, I don't. Just don't get your hopes up."

"I'm afraid hope is all I have at this point. If nothing changes by Tuesday afternoon, I will go home a failure. My sisters are all I have. My sisters and my faith in God. I can't believe our Lord wants Clara in an unhappy marriage any more than I do."

"I respect what you're trying to do, but Joe has lived alone for a long time. He's old and he's set in his ways."

"He has you around every day."

"I'm sort of like Duncan. I'm useful and tolerated because of that."

She shook her head. "You don't know my grandfather nearly as well as you think. He cares deeply about you. He cherishes the hope that you will one day find your way back to God and salvation."

There was no mistaking the sadness that filled Carl's eyes. "Then I reckon you aren't the only one who shouldn't get their hopes up. God isn't interested in my salvation."

He went back into the house and left Lizzie to puzzle

over his words. What had happened to make him lose faith in God's goodness and mercy?

What a strange man Carl King was. He was polite and kind, he liked dogs and children, he was more helpful than most men she knew, and yet he seemed to believe God had abandoned him. Why?

If he had grown up in the Amish faith then surely he must know that God loved all His children. No sin was greater than God's ability to forgive.

With a tired sigh, she unloaded the washer and carried the wet clothes to the line outside. One by one, she hung the shirts, pants, sheets and pillowcases to dry in the fresh morning air until she had filled both clotheslines. She pulled a brown sock out of the basket and then had to search until she found its mate. They had both been neatly darned at the heels. She suspected it was Carl's work. She pinned them together on the clothesline. The next pair she put together had holes in both toes. More mending work for her.

She finished hanging up the load, and as she started for the back steps, movement caught her eye out in the pasture. Carl was striding toward the sheep dotting the far hillside. Duncan stayed close to his side until some unheard command sent him bolting toward the sheep in a wide, sweeping move.

As she watched, her grandfather joined them. The dog gathered the scattered flock into a bunch and began moving them toward the pens just beyond the barn. Carl and the dog worked together until the group was safely penned. After Joe swung the gate shut behind the last ewe, Carl knelt. Duncan raced to him and the two enjoyed a brief moment of play before Carl rose to his feet. He and her grandfather headed farther afield with the dog trotting behind them.

As intriguing as Carl was, she couldn't add him to her list of people to be rescued. First and foremost, she was here to find a home and jobs for herself and her sisters. If there was any chance that her grandfather would change his mind, she had only these few days to prove how valuable she could be and how comfortable a woman in the house could make his life.

She went back to the washing machine and by late afternoon, the pile of clothing had dwindled to a few pieces that she considered rags. The pants that were dry had been folded and laid on her grandfather's bed. His shirts that were clean and mended hung from the pegs along his bedroom wall. The kitchen and bathroom towels had been sorted and put away. The socks that needed mending could wait until after supper. The jeans and shirt she knew were Carl's were piled on a chair in the living room where he was sure to see them.

Eggs from the henhouse and the last of the flour in the bin made a large batch of noodles that she simmered together with some of the canned chicken from the cellar. She discovered two jars of cherries and made an oatmeal-topped cobbler that she hoped would please both the men.

When everything was ready, she walked out onto the porch and rang the dinner bell hanging from one of the posts. A beautiful sunset was coloring the western sky with bands of gold and rose. Such powerful beauty before the darkness of night was another reminder of God's presence at the close of day.

Tomorrow would be a new day and a new chance to find a way to save her sisters.

Bright and early the next morning, Lizzie hurried to get in the buggy, where her grandfather was waiting impatiently. She said, "I hope I have not made us late."

The moment she was seated, Joe slapped the reins against the horse's rump. "Do not expect the horse to make up the time you've lost."

"I don't. Is the service far away?"

"*Nee,* it's less than two miles. It's at the home of Ike and Maggie Mast. I will tell you now that I don't stay for all the visiting and such afterward. We'll go home as soon as the service is over."

"But what about the meal?"

"I eat at home."

Lizzie hid her disappointment. Her family always stayed to eat and visit until late in the afternoon. Sunday service was a huge social event. She had hoped to meet as many local families as possible and see if anyone had work for her. Perhaps she could convince her grandfather to let her stay while he went home. "I would like to meet some of your neighbors and friends. I can walk home after the service."

"No point in getting friendly with people you'll never see again." He kept the horse at a steady trot until they came even with the small shepherd's hut that was set back a little way from the road. He stopped the buggy by the pasture gate and waited.

Lizzie realized he was waiting for Carl. When Carl didn't appear after a few minutes, her grandfather's shoulders slumped ever so slightly. He clicked his tongue and set the horse moving again.

Lizzie glanced back as they drove away. "You were hoping that he would join us."

"He will when he is ready. All things are in God's own time."

"Some people never come back to the Amish life."

"Carl will." He slapped the reins again and the horse broke into a fast trot.

Would Carl ever seek forgiveness, or would he remain an outcast? It seemed so sad. He respected their ways, but something kept him from accepting them. If only she knew more about his past, she might be able to help him, but it wasn't likely she would get to know him that well.

The journey to the preaching service took less than half an hour. When they arrived at the farm home set into the side of a tree-covered hill, Lizzie saw the yard was already filled with buggies. Her grandfather's congregation was a large one. Several young men came to take charge of the buggy and the horse.

Her grandfather got down without waiting for her. Lizzie clasped her hands with trepidation. It was the first time she had attended a prayer meeting at a church besides her own. She wouldn't know anyone here. It was an uncomfortable feeling, but one she was determined to overcome.

Today was for praising God and giving thanks to Him for His blessings.

The singing of the first hymn started by the time they reached the front doors. Inside the house, the living room held four rows of backless wooden benches with a wide center aisle dividing them. The women and girls sat on one side, while the men and boys sat on the other. Her grandfather walked straight ahead to where the married men and elders sat. She made her way to an empty spot on the women's side of the aisle near the back.

She gathered many curious glances. The only face she recognized was the woman from the inn, Naomi Wadler. Smiling and nodding to the woman, Lizzie took a seat and picked up a copy of the Ausbund.

The hymnal was the same one used in the services she attended at home. The weight of the book felt familiar in her hand and gave her a sense of comfort. She might be far from home, but she was never far from God.

When the first hymn ended, she joined in silent prayer with those around her.

Please, Lord, protect and keep my sisters. If it be Your will, let Grandfather change his mind and allow us to live with him. And please, Heavenly Father, help Carl King to find his way back to You. Amen.

When the Sunday prayer service was within walking distance, Carl followed Joe to the neighboring farms. He never went near the buildings, but often, like today, he found a place beneath a tree and settled himself to listen. The sound of solemn voices raised in song came to him on the light spring breeze. The hymns, hundreds of years old, were sung by the Amish everywhere. The words and the meaning remained unchanged by the passage of time. They were as familiar to him as the clothes on his back or the worn boots on his feet.

Sometimes, like now, he softly sang along. The birds added their songs to the praising as the sun warmed the land. Spring was coming. A time of new births, a time of new beginnings. A time for the new lambs to join the flock.

For years, Carl had been waiting for a sign from God that he had been forgiven, that he could return to the fold of worshippers and be clean and whole again, but no sign had been forthcoming.

God had not yet forgiven him for killing a man.

Chapter Five

Lizzie sat patiently through the three-hour-long church service at the home of her grandfather's neighbors, Ike and Maggie Mast. She enjoyed the preaching, singing and prayers. The entire morning lifted her spirits.

When the last notes of the final hymn died away, Lizzie was immediately welcomed by a young woman seated near her, a redhead with a set of freckles that rivaled Lizzie's.

"Hello, and welcome to our church. I'm Sally Yoder. Did I see you arrive with Woolly Joe, or did my eyes deceive me? I didn't know he had any family."

"If you mean Joseph Shetler, then yes, I came with him. I'm his granddaughter from Indiana. I'm Lizzie Barkman."

"Are you Abigail's daughter?" someone asked from behind her. Turning, Lizzie saw it was Naomi Wadler, the woman from the inn.

"*Ja,* my mother's name was Abigail. Did you know her?"

"Very well. No wonder I thought you looked familiar. You resemble her a great deal. How wonderful to see you all grown up. I'm sure you don't remember me, but when you were very young, your mother and I spent many happy hours together. We were dear friends. You have more sisters, don't you?"

"Yes, there are four of us."

"I'm so happy that Joseph has mended the breach with your family. He was deeply saddened when your mother moved away. He never really got over it. I was so sorry to learn of her death. You must come visit me at the inn so that we can catch up. I'd love to hear what Abigail's daughters are doing."

Lizzie didn't care to share information about her strained relationship with her grandfather. Instead, she changed the subject. "I'm still looking for work. Have you heard of anything?"

"I have, and it may be just the thing for you. Come meet Katie and Elam Sutter. Elam's mother mentioned the couple has been thinking of hiring a girl to live in and help with the children and the business."

Excited by the prospect, Lizzie asked, "What kind of business?"

"Elam runs a basket-weaving shop. He and his wife are opening a store to sell their wares here in Hope Springs in addition to taking them to Millersburg to be sold there. We have so many tourists stopping by these days that it makes sense to have a shop locally."

Sally said, "I've worked for Elam for ages, and I've known Katie for several years. They are wonderful people."

Naomi led Lizzie to a group of young mothers seated on a quilt on the lawn. They were keeping an eye on their toddlers playing nearby while several infants slept on the blanket beside them. "Katie, have you found a chore girl yet?" Naomi asked.

Katie picked up a little boy and rose to her feet. She deftly extracted a pebble from his mouth. He yowled in protest. "Jeremiah Sutter, rocks are not for eating. *Nee,* Naomi, I have not found anyone willing to take on my horde."

"They are not a horde. They are adorable. Katie, this is Lizzie Barkman, and she may be just the woman you and Elam are looking for if you don't scare her away."

Lizzie met Katie's gaze and liked what she saw. The young mother had black hair and intelligent dark eyes. Her coloring was a stark contrast to her son's blue-eyed blondness.

"I don't know anything about basket weaving, but I'm willing to learn. I have two younger sisters, so I know something about taking care of children."

Katie put her little boy down and tipped her head slightly as she regarded Lizzie. "You aren't from around here, are you?"

"I was originally. My family moved to Indiana when I was small. My grandfather is Joseph Shetler."

"I didn't realize that Woolly Joe had any family," Katie said.

Sally propped her hands on her hips and rocked back on her heels. "That's exactly what I said."

Naomi smiled sadly at Lizzie. "After your mother and father moved away, your grandfather became a recluse. I hope that will change now."

"I don't believe it will." Lizzie glanced toward the line of buggies. Sure enough, her grandfather was hitching up his horse. He was ready to go. He wouldn't be happy if she kept him waiting.

"I pray that his eyes will be opened and he will see how many of his old friends still care deeply about him and miss him." There was something oddly poignant in Naomi's tone. Lizzie looked at her closely, but Naomi's gaze was fixed on Joe.

After a moment, Naomi sighed and looked back to Katie. "I'll leave you women to get acquainted while I go help set up for the meal. It was wonderful talking to you, Lizzie. I'm serious. You must come by the inn so we can catch up. I want to hear all about Abigail's daughters."

As Naomi walked away, Sally leaned close to Katie. "Did I just hear what I thought I heard?"

Katie wore a puzzled expression, too. "If you just heard Naomi Wadler sighing over Woolly Joe Shetler, then yes."

Lizzie pointed at Katie's son. "Jeremiah just ate another rock."

Katie rolled her eyes. She grabbed her son and swiped a finger through his mouth to pull out a pebble. "Come by our farm on Tuesday of this week and meet my husband. If he agrees, we'll work out the details. How soon could you start?"

"As soon as you would like."

Lizzie could barely contain her excitement. Once she had a job, she would be able to send money home, enough to get all of her sisters to Hope Springs. She had no idea where they would all live, but she put her faith in God. He would provide. She bid the women goodbye and rushed across the yard to where her grandfather was waiting.

A man approached their buggy as they were preparing to leave. "Might I have a word with you, Joe?"

"If it's a short word." Reluctantly, her grandfather nodded toward her. "This is my granddaughter Lizzie Barkman. This fellow is Adrian Lapp."

Adrian smiled at her. "Pleased to meet you. Joe, has Carl King had any experience shearing alpacas?"

Her grandfather scratched his cheek. "I've never heard him mention it."

"But he does all your sheep, right?"

"He does."

"My wife didn't like the man I hired last year. She said he was too rough with them. She's very attached to her animals. I'm looking for someone local who is willing to take on the task."

Joe stroked his beard slowly. "I've heard that they spit on folks."

"Only if they are frightened or very upset. Normally, they are as gentle as lambs."

"I heard the one you call Myrtle spit on the bishop's wife."

Adrian smothered a grin as he glanced over his shoulder. "It was a very unfortunate incident."

To Lizzie's surprise, Joe chuckled. "I would have given a lot to see that."

"Faith would rather the whole thing be forgotten, but a number of people feel as you do. Myrtle spit on me, too, the first time we met. The smell fades in a few days."

"I'll make sure Carl knows that."

"If he's willing to take on the work, just have him drop by tomorrow and let me know. We're in a hurry to get them done, but I know you'll be shearing soon, too. It could wait until after lambing season if need be, but Faith is anxious to get started on a batch of new yarns before our baby arrives. Her orders are already coming in. She's going to need help if she is going to keep up with them."

Lizzie leaned forward. "Are you looking to hire someone?"

Adrian shrugged. "We've been talking about it."

"I have a sister who is looking for work. The pay doesn't have to be much if she can get room and board."

"Does she have experience with carding wool and spinning?"

"She does." It had been years ago, but Lizzie remembered Clara and her mother working together on the big wheel. Before their mother died and Uncle Morris sold it.

"I'll let my wife know. She isn't here today. She wasn't feeling well this morning. Why don't you come over with Carl if he decides he wants the job? That way, you and Faith can discuss it."

"I'll do that." Lizzie didn't want to get her hopes up, but it was a promising lead. She glanced at her grandfather. "Before I go home on the bus."

"Which is Tuesday," he stated.

"But not until in the afternoon," she added. "Please tell your wife I'll stop by even if Carl decides not to take the work."

"All right, I will."

As Adrian walked away, her grandfather turned the buggy and headed down the lane. "I thought I told you to accept your uncle's wishes in the matter of your sister's marriage."

Lizzie remembered Carl's advice and spoke with firm resolve. "I appreciate your wise counsel, but my sister deserves a choice. Nothing good can come from marriage vows made without love."

Joe glanced at her but didn't say anything more. Lizzie relaxed when she realized he didn't intend to argue the point.

It had been a productive morning. So far, the Lord had provided two promising opportunities. Lizzie wasn't going to ignore them. She might be able to offer Clara a job and a place to live, but unless she could find something for all her sisters, Clara wouldn't take it. She wouldn't leave Betsy behind to marry Rufus Kuhns in her stead.

That evening after supper, Joe mentioned Adrian's offer to shear his alpacas to Carl.

Carl remained silent. Lizzie noticed that he didn't rush

into making decisions. He always thought before he spoke. "The extra pay would come in handy. I've never clipped an alpaca, but it can't be too much different than a sheep. I'll give it a try. Can we spare the time tomorrow? We have the sorting pens to build yet."

"We can spare half a day. If we don't get them put together on Monday, Tuesday will be soon enough. Take the job if you want it."

Lizzie broached the subject that couldn't be avoided much longer. "Adrian Lapp cannot do business with you, Carl."

"True, but the man needs help. I'll find a way that is acceptable."

Joe said, "Lizzie will go with you. She can handle the money. Adrian's wife is looking for help with her yarn business."

Carl sat up straighter. "So you may not be leaving?"

"Not if I can find a job and a place to stay."

She thought for a moment that Carl looked happy at the prospect, but he quickly looked away.

Would it please him if she stayed in the area? It shouldn't matter, but for some reason, it did. "The spinning job with Faith Lapp is for my sister Clara. I go Tuesday morning to see if Elam Sutter will hire me to work in his basket-weaving business. It is my hope to bring all my sisters to live here."

Joe pushed his chair back from the table. "The next thing you know, I'm going to be surrounded by a gaggle of women. Well, I won't have it. I like my peace and quiet. You and your sisters can move anywhere you want, so long as you leave me be."

He stomped out of the kitchen and slammed his bedroom door behind him, leaving Carl and Lizzie alone.

"He doesn't mean that." Carl looked embarrassed by the outburst.

She began to gather the dishes. "I think he does. I've done everything I can think of to show him having a woman in his house is a good thing. I've cooked. I've cleaned until my fingers are raw. I've been quiet. I have stayed out of his way to the best of my ability, and still he treats me like a millstone around his neck."

"I appreciate your work, especially your good cooking. I'm sure Joe does, too. I don't think housekeeping skills will impress him enough to let you and your sisters stay here. Joe loves his solitude."

"And you do, too?"

He couldn't meet her gaze. "Yes, I do, too."

She felt so sad for them. They were two lonely men living apart from the world. It seemed that they both planned to remain that way.

Carl woke in the middle of the night bathed in sweat and shaking. He sat up gasping for air. Slowly, his nightmare faded. He wasn't in a grass hut in Africa. He was in a stone shepherd's hut in Ohio.

He had left the door open, and Duncan came in. The dog laid his muzzle on Carl's hand and whined. As soon as Carl's thundering heart slowed, he said, "It's okay, boy."

He had not been forgiven. Every time the events of the past played out in his nightmares, he knew God was reminding him of his sin.

He rose from the bed and got a glass of water. Walking to the door, he looked out at the star-strewn sky and wondered how much more he had to endure.

The events of that terrifying day were as clear to him as the water glass in his hand. He had gone to Africa to be with his sister, Sophia, on her wedding day.

Born with a burning desire to share God's salvation with the world, Sophia chose not to join the Amish faith of her parents, but to become a Mennonite and go out into the world to spread God's word.

His family, like all the Amish, did not believe in seeking converts, but they supported missions of mercy. Sophia's first mission trip took her to Africa. She fell in love with the land and the people, and eventually, with another young missionary. They chose to marry in the village they called home. Sophia wrote and begged that at least one member of her family come to attend her wedding. Carl, being the oldest and unmarried, chose to go.

Although the land and the people were strange, Carl quickly saw why his sister loved the place. He soon became a favorite with some of the village children, particularly a young girl named Christina.

She called him Kondoo Mtu, a name that meant "sheep man" or "shepherd" in her native tongue. His sister told him it was because *ja,* his word for *yes,* sounded like the noise the sheep and goats made. He sometimes wondered if that was why he had decided to stay on Joe's farm and become a true shepherd instead of a carpenter like his father.

The day before Sophia's wedding, Carl had gone out to help Christina find her lost goat when he heard the first gunfire. There had been talk of a civil war, but no one believed it would happen. The frightened child raced back to the camp. Sophia's home was on the edge of the village. Carl caught up with Christina and took her there. When he opened the door, he saw a dozen women from the village huddled together with his sister. The fear in their eyes was terrible to see.

Christina's mother stood up. "Run, Carl. Take my daughter and run away."

Christina began screaming, "Where's Daddy?" She

bolted toward the fighting. Carl raced after her. He saw a dozen villagers lying dead in the street. Christina found the body of her father among them. She sobbed over him and begged him to get up.

As if in slow-motion, Carl saw it all again. A soldier came around the corner and spotted her. He raised his gun. Christina's father's rifle was lying in the dirt at Carl's feet. Carl had grown up hunting. He knew how to use a gun. With barely a thought, he snatched it up and fired.

A second later, he watched the surprise on the soldier's face fade away. The light went out of his eyes as he fell dead.

Carl couldn't get that picture out of his head.

He had killed a man.

Nonviolence was a pillar of the Amish faith. For centuries, they suffered persecution without reprisal as the Bible commanded.

But I say unto you, That ye resist not evil: but whosoever shall smite thee on thy right cheek, turn to him the other also.

It was a creed Carl believed in with all his heart, but his faith hadn't been strong enough. He did not face the death of that child, nor his own certain death, as he should have. God was the giver and taker of life, the judge of men, not Carl King.

He threw down the gun, grabbed Christina and hid as more soldiers scoured the area for him. He managed to make his way back to his sister's home, but he was too late. The women had been found by the soldiers looking for him.

He lived while everyone else died. He should have been brave enough to face his own death as his sister had done, with her Bible in her hands and peace in her soul. Instead, he'd broken a most sacred law: "Thou shalt not kill."

Each morning, he prayed for forgiveness. On those nights when his nightmare didn't come, he began to hope that God had taken pity on him.

But always, like tonight, the nightmare came back. He was forced to watch a man die by his hand over and over again and to know that his actions had cost his sister her life, too.

No, he had not been forgiven.

Later the next morning, Carl loaded his equipment in the back of the wagon and waited for Lizzie. He didn't have to wait long. She came rushing out of the house, still drying her hands on her apron.

She was out of breath by the time she reached him. "I hope I haven't kept you waiting. I had to get the breakfast dishes done and then I had to get something started for Grandfather's lunch. I pray that God wants Clara to work for Faith Lapp. I really do."

Her cheeks were rosy and her eyes sparkled with excitement. How could someone who had been up before dawn and hard at work for hours look so fresh and adorable?

He dismissed the thought as unworthy the moment it occurred. He had no right to look upon an Amish maid with such delight. He laid the reins on the bench seat and scooted over.

Lizzie climbed aboard and picked them up. "You will have to tell me the way."

"Go past the school and turn right at the next road. Then it's about a mile."

"I'm excited to see an alpaca up close. Do they really spit at you? How far can they spit?" She was like a kid on her way to the county fair.

"I have no idea."

"My sister Greta would love to visit a farm with such exotic creatures. She loves animals. She has a special way with them, even the stubborn and mean ones."

"You should write and tell her all about it."

"That is exactly what I will do."

She grew silent and some of the happiness faded from her face.

"What's wrong?" he asked.

"I miss them. I've never been away from them before."

"You will see them again soon enough." He wanted to offer more comfort, a shoulder to cry on if she needed one, but he held himself rigid beside her.

"If I fail to get a job, then I must return home on the bus tomorrow afternoon. As much as I miss them, I don't want to go back and face them having accomplished nothing, for I know my leaving has caused great heartache."

"But it was a brave thing, nonetheless."

Lizzie thought Carl looked tired and sad this morning. She wondered why, but didn't wish to pry. She sensed that he needed comforting. After riding a while in silence, she glanced at him. "Are you okay?"

"I'm fine. I didn't sleep well, that's all."

He just needed cheering up. "I find a cup of herbal tea in the evenings helps me sleep like a babe. I haven't seen any in Grandfather's cupboards, but I'm sure you can buy some in town. I will write down the name for you, if you'd like."

"Thanks."

"If my constant chatter gets on your nerves, just shush me. I can take a hint."

He closed his eyes and rubbed his brow. "A little peace would be nice this morning."

"Absolutely. I understand completely. I often find I'm

not at my best until almost noon. Isn't it a nice morning? March is such a funny month. A person would think winter is over when we have such a pretty day, but then, bang, the cold weather comes back."

"Lizzie."

"What, Carl?"

"Shush."

"Oh. Shush as in stop talking?"

"Is there another kind of shush?"

She opened her mouth, but he held up one hand. "No, don't explain. Shush as in stop talking."

She managed to be quiet for the rest of the trip, but it was hard. How could she cheer him up if she couldn't speak to him?

When they reached the Lapp farm, she met Adrian and Faith's son, Kyle. A nine-year-old boy with bright red hair, freckles and an outgoing personality, he was happy to share his knowledge of shearing alpacas with everyone. Lizzie could have spent all day just gazing at the beautiful, graceful creatures. An adorable baby alpaca, which she learned from Kyle was called a cria, bounced around on stiff legs and darted under the adults standing in a small herd.

Inside the barn where the men were getting ready to work, Kyle indicated a number of bags stacked on nearby hay bales. "These bags are for the fleece. Alpacas have three kinds of fleece. There's prime—that's the best fiber. It's from their back and ribs. The fleece that we get off their thighs, neck and the legs is called seconds. The rest is called thirds and it isn't used by spinners. It's trash, but we keep some for batting inside the cria blankets if the babies are born during cold weather. Our little ones, the ones less than one year old, have prime all over because they've never been shorn."

"Is he bending your ear?" Faith asked as she entered the

barn. She walked with a slight limp and wore a metal brace on her lower leg. Adrian came in with her, leading a white alpaca with a brown-and-white baby trotting at her heels.

"Not at all," Lizzie said with a smile for the boy. "I'm enjoying learning all about your beautiful animals."

The baby came to investigate the hem of Lizzie's dress. She had never seen a more adorable creature. She looked at Faith. "Is it all right if I pet him?"

"Of course. We like to keep the ones we have as tame as possible so that they get used to handling. It makes working with them so much easier. The important thing to remember is that they need to respect humans. We don't make pets of them. An alpaca that is spoiled with a lot of petting and treats can become aggressive when they are grown, especially the males. Once they have lost respect for a human, they can't be trusted."

"It's the same with sheep," Carl said. "It's often the bottle-fed lambs that become the most aggressive ones."

Kyle knelt and gathered the baby in his arms. "This is Jasper."

Lizzie stroked his velvety head. The mother watched them intently and made soft humming sounds to her baby. "I'm afraid I could not raise them. I would constantly want to hug them. They are so soft and they have the most beautiful eyes."

Carl walked around the mother. "If she was a sheep, I'd pick her up and set her on her rump to shear her. With those long legs, that looks a little tricky."

Adrian laughed. "I tried that the first time I attempted to shear Myrtle. She jumped straight up in the air a good four feet off the ground and sent me tumbling backward. Then she spit on me. Don't worry. We have a sock we use for a muzzle now. You'll be safe."

"I have it right here," Faith said and came up to put it on.

Carl tipped his cowboy hat back with one finger. "So how do we do this?"

Adrian led Myrtle forward until she was standing on a large rubber mat. "It's a three-person job. Someone needs to hold her head. That will be me. We put ropes around her legs and just stretch her out until she is flat on the ground. It looks a little awkward, but it doesn't hurt them. I will warn you, some of them really hate this, and they will scream. Others simply lie still until it's all over and never make a sound. Once we have this girl down on the ground, I'll tell you how we need the fleece to be cut. Kyle will gather the blanket as it comes off and put it in the bags. Are you ready to start?"

"As ready as I can get," Carl said with a lack of certainty.

Lizzie watched as Faith wrapped loops around each of Myrtle's legs, then she and Kyle pulled on the ropes until Myrtle was lying on her belly. Several of the other alpacas wandered over to watch what was happening. Having them and her baby nearby kept Myrtle quiet.

Carl followed Adrian's instructions and quickly learned the best way to shear the animal. In a matter of a few minutes, Myrtle was released and scrambled to her feet.

Lizzie giggled. "She looks positively ridiculous."

Myrtle's big woolly body was now skinny and scrawny except for the thick fleece that had been left around her head and a pom-pom at the end of her tail.

Kyle grabbed the rest of the fleece from the floor around Myrtle's feet. "They always looked shocked. Like, what just happened to me?"

Lizzie met Carl's gaze, and they both chuckled. He said, "She looks like that is exactly what she's thinking."

"Are you from Texas?" Kyle asked.

Lizzie perked up. Perhaps she would learn something about Carl's past today.

Carl frowned. "What makes you think that?"

Kyle pointed to his head. "Your cowboy hat. I'm from Texas. Lots of people wear hats like yours out there."

Kyle was from Texas? Lizzie glanced at his parents. Faith smiled and said, "*Ja,* our boy is a Texan. Confusing, isn't it? Tell them how you came to live in Ohio, Kyle."

The little boy grew solemn and crossed his arms over his chest. "It went like this. My dad, my first dad, was my aunt Faith's brother. He moved away from his Amish family and married my first mom. I was born in Texas. Are you with me? Then they died in a car accident. After that, I was really scared and sad. I lived in this home with other kids without parents.

"I didn't like it much, but I did like my foster mom. Her name was Becky. Anyway, a social-worker lady brought me here to Ohio to live with my aunt Faith. Then we met Adrian. He had the farm next to our house. Only, it's our farm now, and someone else lives in my aunt's house. A nice fellow named Gideon Troyer and his wife, Rebecca. He used to be a pilot.

"Anyway, Adrian became my new dad because he fell in love with my aunt and married her and they adopted me, so now they are my new *mamm* and *daed.* And that's how I got to be Amish.

"I do miss having a TV, but I like having alpacas a lot. I have one named Shadow. He's black as coal, and I get to keep all the money from his fleece when we sell it." Kyle's solemn expression dissolved into a wide grin.

Lizzie struggled to take in all of the information he had dished out so quickly. Faith laughed. "Did you get that?"

"I think so. Kyle is from Texas."

Adrian handed the lead rope to the boy. "Take Myrtle back to the pen and bring one of the others."

Kyle rushed to do as he had been asked. He was a charming child, but Lizzie was disappointed that she hadn't learned anything about where Carl was from.

Would she ever?

Chapter Six

Carl soon relaxed and grew more confident with each animal he sheared. As Adrian had said, some of the animals screamed in protest, but most lay quietly and allowed him to do his job without worrying about injuring them. He was spit at once but managed to jump aside, and only his boot took a direct hit. After that, Faith put muzzles on every animal.

Lizzie, of course, dissolved into laughter as he scraped his boot clean on a nearby hay bale. Each time she caught him looking at her after that, she pinched her nose and made a face.

He tried to keep his attention strictly on the task at hand, but having Lizzie working beside him made that difficult.

Her good humor never lagged as she pitched in to help without being asked. She was soon tying up alpacas as if she'd been doing it for years. When one was a particularly bad squirmer, Lizzie lay down on the ground beside him to help hold the animal still.

When she wasn't needed to help control the animals, she was helping to sort and bag the fleece. The whole time, she was smiling and cheerful, chuckling at the antics of the alpacas and making the morning one of the most pleasant he'd had in a long time.

When noon rolled around, Faith brought a picnic hamper down from the house. Lizzie followed with a large quilt over her arm and a pitcher of lemonade in her hand.

"Lizzie suggested we eat out here. I think a picnic is a wonderful idea. It's the first one of the year," Faith said as Adrian took the hamper from her.

Lizzie glanced at Carl and then looked away. "It's such a beautiful spring day that I thought it would be a shame to spend it eating at the table inside."

"Adrian, would you spread the quilt in a sunny place for us?" Faith indicated the spot she wanted and her husband quickly did as she asked.

Within a few minutes, they were all settled on the quilt except for Carl. He carried a bale of hay out and put it where he could sit and lean against the trunk of an apple tree.

Faith withdrew a plate full of ham sandwiches made with thick slices of homemade bread from the hamper. They all helped themselves as Lizzie poured glasses of fresh lemonade. She handed them out to everyone except Carl. When she approached, he was busy wiping his hands with a wet towel. "Just set it on the ground. I'll get it in a minute."

She caught his glance and nodded. It was acceptable.

"When do you plan to start shearing Joe's sheep?" Adrian asked.

"Tomorrow."

"How many sheep does Joe have?" Kyle asked as he examined the large clippers Carl had laid aside.

"He has four rams and about two hundred ewes."

Kyle's eyes widened. "And I thought shearing ten alpacas was a lot of work. How long will it take you?"

"If the weather holds and nothing goes wrong, we'll be done in three or four days."

Kyle was holding Carl's shears trying to squeeze the big scissor-like blades together. "Doesn't your hand get tired?"

Carl almost choked on his lemonade. "It does. By the end of the week, my hand is very tired. I'll show you how to use those. A good shearer can earn a tidy sum of cash in the spring."

Kyle handed them back. "No, thanks. I'm gonna farm with my dad and grow peaches. How did you learn? Did your dad shear sheep?"

"*Nee,* my father is a carpenter." A sharp stab of regret hit Carl. He hadn't seen his father since he left home when he was twenty-four years old. He would be twenty-nine this fall. Five years was a long time. When would he be able to go home? When would God grant him the forgiveness he craved?

"Where does he work?" Lizzie asked softly.

"Pennsylvania." He didn't share more details. "Lizzie mentioned you are looking for a spinner to work with you, Faith."

Faith smiled. "Lizzie has a sister who might be interested in the job."

"My oldest sister, Clara. She used to spin with our mother, but that was many years ago."

"Did she like it?" Adrian asked.

"She loved doing it, but our uncle sold the spinning wheel after our mother died."

Adrian pushed his straw hat back a little and regarded her intently. "Is she staying with Joe, too?"

"*Nee.* Clara is at home in Indiana, but I know she would come if she knew she had a job."

Adrian gave Faith a speaking glance and then said, "I would rather meet your sister first and see her skill level before we offer her a job. Faith's work has gained a good reputation among the shops that purchase her yarns. We don't want to start selling an inferior product."

Lizzie nodded. "I understand. It's just that it's very important that Clara have a job soon."

"And why is that?" Adrian asked.

Lizzie looked to Carl. He was pleased that she valued his opinion. He nodded. "Tell them."

She drew a deep breath. "My uncle is making Clara marry a cruel man. Rufus Khuns is our landlord. We live and work on his dairy farm. Clara doesn't want to marry him, but Onkel Morris is afraid Rufus will turn us out if she doesn't. He told Clara that he'll make our youngest sister wed Rufus if Clara won't. Betsy is barely seventeen."

"That's terrible. Oh, Adrian, we have to help them," Faith cried.

Adrian took his wife's hand in his and patted it. "Calm yourself. Remember, the midwife said getting upset isn't good for your blood pressure."

"I know. And sitting for a long time at the wheel makes my feet swell, so I shouldn't do that, either. I will be glad when this babe makes an appearance."

Adrian turned to Lizzie. "Tell your sister she has a job here for as long as she needs one."

"But what about your other sisters?" Faith asked. "They can't stay and be abused in your uncle's home."

"I have a job interview tomorrow at Elam Sutter's home. Once Clara and I both have jobs, we'll be able to take care of our little sisters. I don't care what it takes. I won't leave them behind."

Faith reached over and squeezed Lizzie's hand. "Of course you can't. I will pray for the success of your mission every day."

* * *

Lizzie felt as if she had finally found people who understood what she faced. It was a deeply comforting feeling.

She and Faith carried the quilt and lunch items back to the house as the men returned to shear the final four alpacas. After the dishes were washed, Faith said, "Come see my spinning room. You will want to tell your sister about where she'll be working."

She led the way to a bright room that had been built off the kitchen on the east side of the house. In it were three spinning wheels of various sizes and dozens of skeins of yarn. The windows overlooked a small orchard where the shorn alpacas were gathering beneath the trees.

Lizzie admired the largest spinning wheel. "This is the kind that my mother had. What a lovely place you have to work."

"Adrian built it for me when I first moved here. He knew how much I liked to watch my animals."

"He seems like a caring husband."

Faith cupped her hands over her pregnant belly. "He is a wonderful man. I never thought I would find someone like him. My first husband was a very demanding and hard man. Life was not…easy with him. It wasn't all his fault. He had a very tragic childhood. Then we had two little daughters who were stillborn early in our marriage, and he was never the same after that."

"I'm so sorry for your loss."

"*Danki.* I know they are with God in Heaven and I will see them again someday. You must tell your sister not to give up hope and not to marry without love. God brings special people into our lives exactly when we need them. If it is His will, your sister will find a man like my Adrian, and she will know the joy of being a true wife."

"I will tell her. Thank you for giving her a job. I can't

believe how fortunate I've been since coming to Hope Springs."

"I felt the same way when I first arrived. So many people came to give me a hand getting my house and my farm in order. My husband and I had moved around a lot, so I'd never known the sense of community that exists here. You and your sisters will see. You'll be welcome by all."

"I hope so."

"You have not mentioned how Joe feels about your sisters coming here. Is he glad? I have only known him as the recluse who shuns the company of all others except for Carl."

"Grandfather doesn't want us here."

"How sad for you."

"Honestly, I think it is sad for him."

"You're right. We can't change how people feel. We can only do what we know to be right, and bringing your sisters here sounds right to me."

"Bless you for understanding."

"I do. Now, we must get back to the shearing or I'll find black thirds mixed in with my white firsts." She chuckled. "I have good men, but they still need supervision."

It didn't take long to finish shearing the rest of the animals. Faith led the last one back to their enclosure while Adrian pulled a wallet from his pocket.

He counted out the amount and held it toward Carl. "My wife is very satisfied with your work. I hope I can count on you for next year."

"If I'm still in the area. Give the money to Lizzie while I go wash up. They might be prized for their fleece, but it makes me itch." Carl walked to a nearby stock tank and began to rinse his arms.

Adrian seemed a bit surprised, but offered the payment to Lizzie. She accepted it and put it in her pocket.

Later, back at her grandfather's farm, she left the bills on the table and went down to the cellar for a jar of vegetables. When she came up, the money was gone. Carl had been as good as his word. Everything had been done carefully so as not to have Adrian or Faith unknowingly break their church's Ordnung.

Once again, Lizzie was puzzled by Carl's behavior. Adrian and Faith had no idea that Carl was a shunned person. He could have gone about his business as an Englischer and no one would've been the wiser. Why did he take such great care to protect the people when he was no longer a member of their faith? If he cared so much, why didn't he ask forgiveness for his sin, whatever it was, and be welcomed into the church again?

It didn't make sense. Nothing about Carl made sense. And yet she spent a great deal of time thinking about him and wishing she could find a way to help.

When her grandfather came in for supper that evening, he hung his hat on the peg by the door as usual. "Carl won't be joining us."

"Why not?" She set a platter of noodles on the table.

"Said he wasn't hungry. How did the alpaca shearing go?"

"Fine. Is Carl unwell?"

"Not that I could see."

"Is it unusual for him to miss a meal?"

"He's a grown man. If he doesn't want to eat, he doesn't want to eat. Could be he's tired of your cooking."

She snatched the dish off the table. "There's nothing wrong with my cooking. If you don't want it, I'll feed yours to the dog."

"I never said I didn't want it," he admitted grudgingly.

She glared at him. "I'm a good cook."

"I said that before, didn't I?"

"Then you shouldn't suggest otherwise. It's hurtful."

It took him a few seconds, but finally, he said, "I didn't mean to hurt your feelings. Now can I eat?"

It was as close to an apology as she was likely to get. She set the platter on the table again and turned away to hide a smile. Her grandfather needed someone to stand up to his cantankerous ways. Carl was right about that.

She went to the window and looked out, but she couldn't see his hut beyond the barn. "Carl was quiet on the ride home from the Lapp farm. I didn't give it much thought. I assumed he was tired, but perhaps he was ill."

"I hope not. We need to get started on our beasts first thing in the morning. The lambs are due to start arriving in two to three weeks."

"I hope I can be here to see it." She turned around and went back to the table. "I remember watching the new lambs when I was little. They jumped, ran and played with each other, and it looked like they were having so much fun. Mother said they were leaping with joy."

"Did she?"

"She said the lambing season was the hardest work of the year, but it was all worth it."

A sad, faraway look came into his eyes. "*Ja,* my girl was right about that."

He bowed his head to pray and didn't speak again during the meal. He went to his room directly afterward, leaving Lizzie alone. Perhaps she had been wrong to mention her mother in front of him. It seemed to bring him pain.

She went to bed that night and lay under the quilt her mother had made. Outside her open window, a chilly breeze blew by and carried the sounds of the night with it. An owl hooted nearby. In the distance, a sheep bleated and another answered. A dog barked somewhere.

This was her last night in the house where her mother

had grown up. Tomorrow, if she got the job with Elam Sutter, she would stay with his family and work to bring her sisters to Hope Springs. If she wasn't hired, she would be forced to go home, back to Indiana. At least she'd found a job for Clara, but she wasn't sure her sister would take it if it meant leaving the rest of them.

She slipped out of bed and got to her knees. "Please, Lord, I'm begging You. Give me the strength and wisdom to find a place for all of us."

Knowing that she could do nothing more and that it was all in God's hands, she climbed into bed and quickly fell asleep.

Lizzie finished her chores the next morning and hurried outside. She was surprised to see Carl waiting with the pony already hitched to the cart. "*Danki,* Carl, but you should not do this for me."

"It's not a favor, Lizzie. It's part of the work I do here. Do you know how to get where you're going?"

"I have a general idea."

"I drew a map. It's on the seat if you need it."

"That was very thoughtful of you."

"Good luck. I hope you get the job."

"I shall know soon enough." She stood beside the cart knowing that she should hurry, but she was reluctant to actually get under way.

What if it didn't work out? What if she was back here in two hours to pack and board the bus this afternoon? The thought was depressing.

Carl stepped close to her. "The journey of a thousand miles begins with a single step."

"I thought I took that first step when I walked out of my uncle's house last week."

"Then you are well on your way to where you want to be. This next step cannot be as difficult as that one."

She smiled softly. "You are right about that. You are right about a lot of things, Carl King."

"And I will be right if I tell you to hurry up and go or you won't get back in time to make us lunch."

She laughed. "I declare, you men think with your stomachs."

"I'm going to miss your cooking, Lizzie Barkman."

"I'm going to miss cooking for you."

"You will have Sundays off if Sutter gives you the job. Feel free to come out here and cook to your heart's content."

"That is only if I get the job."

"I don't know Elam Sutter, but he is a fool if he doesn't hire someone as hardworking as you are. Now, get going. Joe and I need to get our sheep sheared."

Lizzie climbed into the cart and picked up the reins. "At least you know they won't spit on you. See you soon."

She slapped the reins against the pony and left Carl standing in the yard watching her. When she reached the end of the lane, she looked back. She lifted a hand and waved. Carl saw her gesture and waved back.

Lizzie drove toward town with a light heart that had nothing to do with a job prospect. Her happy mood was because Carl cared about her comfort and because he said he would miss her if she left.

Lizzie arrived at the Sutter farm and was immediately welcomed by a little girl about four years old, followed by a puppy that reminded Lizzie of Duncan.

"Guder mariye," the little girl called out. She turned and shouted toward the house, "Mamm, we have company."

Lizzie stepped down from the cart. "Thank you. You must be Rachel."

"*Ja,* I am. Who are you?"

"My name is Lizzie Barkman, and I'm here to see your father about a job."

"Papa is in his workshop. Shall I get him?"

"That would be nice, *danki.*"

The little girl turned to her puppy and patted her leg. "Come on, Peanut Butter. Let's go find Papa."

Together they ran toward the barn. Lizzie heard the door of the house open and saw Katie come out with Jeremiah balanced on her hip. "Lizzie, I'm so glad you are here. Come in the house. My husband should be in shortly."

"Rachel just went to tell him that I'm here."

"Oh, *goot.* She is quite the little helper. She makes me wish for another girl. She is much less trouble than my boys have been."

"What has Jeremiah tried to swallow today?"

"My sewing bobbin. I can't take my eyes off him for a minute. Thankfully, the baby isn't much trouble yet, but I'm sure he'll be just like his brother when he is old enough to get into mischief."

Lizzie held out her arms for Jeremiah and was delighted when he grinned and reached for her in return. She propped him on her hip and followed Katie into the house. They were settled at the kitchen table when Elam came in. He hung his hat on a peg by the door.

Jeremiah, who until that moment had been quiet seated on Lizzie's lap, started whining to get down. Elam plucked him away from Lizzie.

"Charming the girls already, are you?" Elam took a seat at the table and allowed the little boy to sit on his lap.

"Indeed, he has been," Lizzie replied.

"My wife tells me you are interested in working for us. Have you any experience at basket weaving?"

"None, but I would be interested to learn. I can help with the children, of that I'm certain."

"Well, then, come down to the shop and let me show you what you will need to know. You may decide the work isn't for you. It can be tedious."

He handed his son to his wife, and Lizzie followed him outside and into his shop. It was part of the barn, but had been walled off to separate it from the rest of the structure. The moment Lizzie stepped inside the room, the aromatic scent of cedar and wood shavings enveloped her. The walls had been painted a bright white. Tools hung from the pegs neatly arranged on one wall. A long table sat in the middle of the workshop, and a small stove in one corner held a simmering vat of something reddish-brown. Around the table sat three women, each with partially completed baskets in front of them.

Elam said, "This is Mary, Ruby and Sally. They all work for me part-time."

Sally put down the basket she was working on. "Lizzie, how nice to see you again."

Lizzie met the other women, who, as it turned out, were Elam's sister and sister-in-law. After seeing how they turned the thin strips of poplar wood into beautiful baskets, Lizzie realized this was something she would like to learn. She thanked the women for their demonstrations, asked a few questions and then followed Elam back to the house.

Katie was setting out mugs of coffee. Everyone took a seat at the kitchen table. "Well, what did you think?" Katie asked.

"I think I have a lot to learn, but it looks like something I would enjoy."

"How soon would you be able to start?" Elam asked.

"Today," Lizzie said quickly.

Elam and Katie exchanged amused glances.

"I'm afraid I don't have a room ready for you yet," Katie said.

"Why don't you start tomorrow? If you think you'll like the work, let's give it a two-week trial," Elam suggested.

Lizzie grinned as excitement bubbled up inside her. She took a sip of coffee. "Tomorrow will be fine."

Carl secured the last panel into place with a length of wire and glanced out the barn door to see Lizzie returning. Even from across the yard, he could see the grin on her face. She caught sight of him and jumped down from the cart. "I got the job," she yelled.

He couldn't believe how relieved he was. She wouldn't be going back to Indiana. She had a job and a place to stay in the neighborhood. He would see her again. Even if only from a distance.

Joe came up to stand beside him. "What did she say?"

"She said she got the job."

Joe gave a disgusted humph and walked away, but Carl wasn't fooled. Joe might not admit it, but he didn't want her to leave, either.

A few minutes later, Lizzie came out of the house and raced down the lane with something in her hand. Intrigued, Carl watched until she slipped whatever she was carrying into the mailbox and raised the flag to let the mail carrier know there was mail to pick up. Was it a letter to her sisters? Probably.

Carl hoped everything would work out for them, but he knew what people desired was not always what God had planned for them. His poor little sister's short life was proof of that.

Turning back to his work, Carl began getting ready to

shear. He had three days of hard work ahead of him. He wouldn't get much done if he couldn't stop thinking about Lizzie. He didn't need the constant distraction of having her near, but…oh, how he desired it.

After spending much of yesterday in her company, he had retreated to his hut, thinking that the distance would help him stop thinking about her. It hadn't worked.

The mixture of foolish longing and painful reality swirling through his brain left him feeling hopelessly muddled.

Lizzie had a way of turning him inside out with just a smile. How was he going to get through another day, let alone the years ahead, if she stayed in Hope Springs?

Lizzie could barely control her excitement as she walked back from the mailbox. Everything was falling into place. The letter she mailed to Mary contained a second letter to her sisters explaining everything: Lizzie's job, Clara's job and her fervent hope that they would all be together soon.

In with the letter, Lizzie had put all of her money. It was enough for a one-way ticket for Clara. She prayed that Clara would come. Together, they would soon earn enough to pay for Betsy and Greta to join them and keep the younger women from being forced into marriage instead. It wasn't a foolproof plan, but it was all Lizzie had to offer.

What they needed now was a place to stay. The Lord had provided jobs. Lizzie was sure He would provide them with a home, too. She just had to have faith.

Bubbling with happiness and optimism, she went to the barn to watch the men at work. A small group of sheep had been gathered in a pen inside the barn. The air was filled with sounds of their bleating as they milled around. A narrow passageway had been built from the large pens outside to a smaller one where Carl was preparing to start the work.

A large piece of plywood had been put on the ground outside the gate of the smallest pen. Carl was down on one knee on the board tying on wool moccasins. When he finished, he reached for the clippers and affixed them to his right hand.

Moving closer, Lizzie said, "Why the special shoes?"

"They keep my feet dry and keep me from slipping on the oils from the fleece."

"Are you going to shear the rams first?" She eyed the four big fellows separated in a pen by themselves.

"That's right." Carl didn't look at her but kept his eyes downcast.

"Why?"

"They're bigger and harder to work with. It's best to get them out of the way so the rest of the work goes more easily. We only have four rams. It doesn't normally take long."

"And you said two hundred ewes." It sounded like a tremendous amount of work for one man and her elderly grandfather.

"That's right."

"I vaguely remember watching the shearing when I was little. A man used electric clippers. He brought his own generator with him. I thought it was very worldly at the time. Doesn't it take longer to clip the fleece by hand?"

Unlike the clippers she remembered, Carl had what looked like a giant pair of scissors strapped to his hand. The blades hooked together at the handle ends instead of in the center.

"It takes me about six minutes per sheep instead of four minutes if I were to use electric clippers. Joe likes them shorn the old way."

"In keeping with our faith. That's understandable."

"He likes it because the fleece isn't cut so close to the skin. Hand-sheared sheep are left with a short coat instead of looking naked. It gives them better protection against foul weather. It's also less stressful for our pregnant mothers without the buzzing sound of the clippers and the smell of gasoline fumes from a generator."

"Are the two of you gonna keep yacking or can we get some work done?" Joe shouted from just outside the pen where the sheep were milling.

Carl waved. "I'm ready."

"What do you need me to do?" she asked.

"There needs to be a clear flow of sheep entering and leaving the shearing area. This barn is divided into two parts. Where the sheep come in and where they go out. The catch pen, the small one here, is connected to the outside corrals by movable panels."

"I see that." The narrow alleyway was just wide enough for one single ram to walk down to the actual shearing pen.

"After I'm done shearing the sheep, I'll turn him into this second alley. I need you to close the gate behind him so he can't run back into this area."

"Got it."

"Once I'm done with all of them, you'll need to close that big gate by the barn door and open the smaller gate beside it so the ewes go out to a separate corral."

"So you just want me to chase them outside for you?"

"Basically. Don't get in with the rams. They can be mean."

"I will remember that."

"Joe may need help giving the animals their worm medicine while I have them still. He'll take care of the fleece that's cut off, too. You can make notes in our logbook for us. Each sheep has an ear tag with a number on it. Joe will tell you what to write."

"Sounds easy enough."

"It is if the sheep cooperate. The only thing they do without protest is grow wool. Ready to start?"

"Sure."

Lizzie quickly learned that sheep were not the cute, cuddly animals of her memory. They were much stronger than they looked, horribly stubborn, smelly and incredibly loud. The bleating grew to a deafening din inside the barn.

Duncan nipped at the heels of the rams as the reluctant animals filed into the catch pen.

Carl opened a small gate and pulled out the first struggling ram. Grasping the heavy wool, he tipped the sheep backward until it was sitting. The second the sheep's feet were all off the ground, it stopped struggling. The animal looked as if it were being held still by the force of Carl's will.

With the ram braced between his legs, Carl quickly set to work clipping first the belly fleece and then around the entire animal until the wool came off in one large piece.

Joe pulled the fleece aside, folded it and placed it on a nearby table. He made a few quick notes in a ledger, gave the animal a dose of medicine and then went to move the next ram into the catch pen with Duncan's help.

Lizzie watched how it was all being done as Carl sheared his second ram. She noticed the first ram had come back inside to be with the others. While Joe was busy rolling up the fleece, she went to shoo the fellow outside.

The ram balked and wouldn't leave. She opened the gate to go in and move him along. In the next second, she realized her mistake. The ram, seeing a new way out, bolted past her, knocking the gate wide open.

Lizzie cried out a warning, but it was too late. The ram didn't slow down. He plowed into Joe and sent him flying before charging through the open barn door beyond. She stared in horror at her grandfather's crumpled figure as Carl raced to his side.

Chapter Seven

Lizzie drove the buggy as fast as she dared. Carl sat in the back cradling Joe, but with every bounce and jolt, her grandfather moaned in pain. The sound made her cringe with remorse. It was all her fault. In her foolish need to prove she could be useful, she'd simply proven she was careless.

After what seemed like an eternity, the outskirts of Hope Springs came into view. Thankfully, there was very little traffic on the streets. She was able to follow Carl's directions and they arrived within a few minutes at the front doors of the Hope Springs Medical Clinic.

Carl lifted Joe out of the buggy and carried him inside. The tiny, elderly receptionist behind the desk jumped to her feet. "Oh, my. What has happened?"

"Joe's been hurt bad," Carl said.

"Bring him this way. I'll get the doctor."

Carl and Lizzie followed her down a short hallway and into an examination room. Carl gently laid Joe on the bed. "It's okay, Joe. You're going to be fine."

A young man in a white lab coat hurried into the room. "I'm Dr. Zook. What seems to be the matter?"

"Where is Dr. White?" Carl asked.

"He's not in today. I'm his partner. Is that a problem?"
Carl shook his head.

"Are you related to Bishop Zook?" Lizzie asked.

"Very distantly, if at all. Zook is simply a common name in these parts."

Outside the door, the receptionist asked, "Should I call for an ambulance, Doctor?"

"Give me a few minutes to see how serious this is, Wilma. Have Amber finish with Mrs. Lapp and then ask her to join me. Can someone tell me what happened?"

"It's my fault." Lizzie clasped her hands together. "I left one of the gates open and a ram got out. He ran into Grandfather and knocked him down. Grandfather hit his head on one of the steel fence posts. It was bleeding terribly."

The doctor began to unwind Lizzie's apron from around Joe's head. "Head wounds are notorious for bleeding a lot. Has he been unconscious long?"

Carl took a step back from the bed to give the doctor more room. "He's been in and out for the past half hour or so. He complains that his right leg hurts. I think it's broken."

The doctor looked kindly at Lizzie. "You might want to step out and let us get him undressed. I'll let you know the extent of his injuries as soon as I've finished examining him."

Lizzie nodded and left the room. She found her way back to the waiting area. Taking a seat on one of the upholstered chairs that lined the wall, she put her head in her hands and prayed.

A short time later, she heard a door open and she looked up. It wasn't the doctor. It was a blonde Englisch woman in a pale blue smock. She walked beside Faith Lapp.

"Everything looks good with your pregnancy, Faith. I'll see you back in two weeks. Sooner if you have any problems. You know I'm available day or night. I'd love to stay and chat a little longer, but I'm needed for another patient."

"*Danki,* Amber. I will see you in two weeks," Faith said. She turned to leave and caught sight of Lizzie. Her eyes widened with surprise. "Lizzie, what are you doing here?"

"Grandfather has been hurt."

"I'm so sorry to hear that. Is it serious?" She sat down beside Lizzie and took her hand.

Her comforting gesture was all that was needed to push Lizzie's shattered emotions over the edge. She burst into tears.

Faith wrapped an arm around Lizzie's shoulder. "There, there, don't cry. He is in God's hands, and God is good."

Lizzie nodded but couldn't speak. She was too choked with tears and worry.

Faith stayed with her until the doctor finally came out to talk to her. She could tell by the look on his face that it wasn't good news. She rose to her feet. "How is he?"

"He's resting comfortably at the moment. I've given him something for pain. The head wound was not serious. It required a few stitches, but he did sustain a minor concussion. The problem is that Joe has a broken hip. We can't treat that here. He needs to go to the hospital. He'll need surgery to pin the broken pieces together."

"Surgery? Is that dangerous at his age?" Faith asked.

"All surgery comes with risks, but I'm afraid there's very little choice. The fracture won't heal unless it can be immobilized."

"Do what you think is best, Doctor. Can I see him now?"

"Of course. I'll make arrangements for an ambulance to transport him to the hospital in Millersburg."

Faith laid a hand on Lizzie's arm. "I'll let Bishop Zook

know what has happened. Don't worry. Everything will be taken care of."

Lizzie nodded and walked down the hall, but hesitated before going into the room. What could she say except that she was sorry? She wiped the tears from her cheeks and opened the door.

Joe lay on the same bed with his eyes closed. A sheet was pulled up to his chin. A white bandage stood out starkly on his forehead. He looked pale and helpless.

Carl sat in a chair beside him. He glanced up as Lizzie peered in. "It's okay. He's awake."

"Of course I'm awake," Joe growled. "Who could sleep with all this commotion?"

"Oh, Daadi, I'm so sorry. I was only trying to help. Please forgive me."

"Things happen. That old ram has had it in for me since I bought him. Carl, it will be up to you to get the shearing done. It'll be hard to do it all yourself."

"I can handle it, Joe. You just rest and get better."

"You won't be able to manage the lambing alone."

Lizzie stepped closer to the bed. "I'll help. I know I made a mess of things today, but I want to make it up to you."

"What about your new job?" Carl asked.

"I'm sure when the Sutters hear what's happened, they will understand if I can't start work for a few more days."

"It will be a few weeks."

"Oh."

Joe shifted uncomfortably on the bed. "The girl won't be any use to you, Carl."

"She'll be better than no one."

It wasn't much of a recommendation, but Lizzie was thankful that he spoke up for her. "Faith Lapp is out in the waiting room. She said she'll let Bishop Zook know what has happened."

Joe pushed up on one elbow, his eyes blazing. "I don't want that busybody Esther Zook in my house, do you hear me?"

Lizzie was stunned by his outburst. Carl rose and eased Joe back on the bed. "I thought you liked the bishop. You told me he was a good man."

"He's a good man married to a shrew of a woman. She'll turn her nose up at everything I own and tell folks what a pity it is that I've let the place go to ruin. I don't want her to set foot inside my door."

Lizzie moved to stand beside him on the other side of the bed. "I won't let her in. I promise."

The outside door opened and the nurse entered. "The ambulance is here. I'm going to have you both step into the waiting room while they get Mr. Shetler ready for transport. Which one of you is going to ride with him?"

"I will," Lizzie said quickly.

"*Nee,* you go home. I want Carl to come."

Lizzie had to concede. Of course he wanted his friend, not the careless granddaughter he barely knew who put him here in the first place.

The nurse gestured to Lizzie to come with her. When they were outside in the hallway, she said, "We haven't met. I'm Amber White. I'll make arrangements for a driver to take you to the hospital."

Embarrassed, Lizzie shook her head. "I have no money to pay a driver."

"Don't worry about that. We have a fund set up for just such an emergency. All the local Amish churches donate to it. The driver will make sure you get to the hospital and that you get home when you are ready. Just let the receptionist have your name and address."

"I don't know how to thank you."

"Of course you do. Someday, you will see a person in need, and you will help them. That is all the thanks I require." Amber went back to the room and Lizzie went to speak to the woman behind the desk.

Carl rode in the back of the ambulance strapped into a small seat out of the way of the crew, but situated where he could see Joe. His friend's color was so pale that Carl began to worry something else was wrong. At the hospital, Carl stood aside and tried to keep out of the way as they admitted Joe and readied him for surgery.

When a lull in the activity finally occurred, the two men were alone for a few minutes.

Joe looked over at him. "With that long face, you make a man think you're on your way to a funeral."

"It will be a long time before anyone plants you in the ground, Woolly Joe."

"I hope so, but a man never knows what the good Lord has in store for him. Could be that I'm on my way to see Him now and just don't know it."

"Lizzie feels bad enough. If you decide to die, she's gonna feel awful."

"She should go stay with the Sutters instead of staying on the farm."

"If you are worried about her safety or anything else, don't be."

"No, it isn't that. I know you'll watch over her. I have no worries on that score. It's just that a sheep farm isn't any place for a woman."

"You don't give Lizzie enough credit. She can handle the work and then some."

"I bought the place a year before I married Lizzie's grandmother. My wife, Evelyn, hated it. She hated the sheep. She hated the smell of them. She hated the long hours and the hard work during the lambing season. I thought she would grow to love it as I did, but that never happened. After a few years, I realized it wasn't the farm. She was never happy with me."

"I'm sorry to hear that."

"The Lord didn't bless us with a child until we were close to thirty. I thought having a baby on the place would make a difference to Evelyn, but it didn't. She died when Abigail was only two. I didn't want the girl to grow up hating the place the way her mother did. I sent her to live with my wife's sister until she was fourteen. I visited her every week, but I'm not sure it was enough. Maybe if I had kept her with me from the start, she would've felt differently about leaving the way she did. Maybe she thought I didn't care about her, but I did. I loved my little girl."

Carl laid a hand on his friend's shoulder. "Joe, if you give Lizzie half a chance, she will grow to love you as I do."

Joe shook his head. "It's better to be alone. You take care of my sheep while I'm laid up, you hear me?"

"I hear you. The sheep will be fine."

"I know they will be with you looking out for them. You and I, we get along okay. We don't need anyone else."

Carl had spent the past five years believing that was true, but now he wasn't so sure. He was learning that a life spent alone could be painfully lonely.

A nurse in surgical garb entered the room. "Mr. Shetler, your granddaughter is here. Would you like to see her before we take you to surgery?"

"*Nee,* let's get this over with."

The nurse looked surprised, but said, "I'll show her where the waiting room is."

A few minutes later, more people came in. Joe was

wheeled from the room. Carl followed them to a large set of double doors.

One of the nurses gestured toward a side hall. "The waiting room is the first door on the left. The surgeon will come talk to you as soon as he is finished."

Carl laid a hand on Joe's arm and leaned close. "God is with you, my friend."

"I know. I just hope He is with the Englisch *doktor,* too."

Carl managed a smile. When they took Joe through the double doors, he walked down to the waiting room.

Lizzie was seated alone by the window. Her hands were clasped together and her eyes were closed. He knew that she was praying. As if she sensed his presence, she looked up and rose to her feet. "How is he?"

"They just took him into surgery."

She sank back onto her chair. "He didn't want to see me."

"Don't dwell on it. When he gets out of here, you can ply him with more of your wonderful cherry cobbler."

"I don't think my cooking can undo the damage I've done today. Do you?"

He didn't have an answer for that.

They waited together in silence until the surgeon finally came in to tell them Joe's surgery had gone well. Later, when Joe was moved to a room, he refused any visitors. Carl, knowing Joe wouldn't change his mind about seeing her, convinced Lizzie to go home.

By the time the driver delivered them to the farm, it had grown dark. Carl stood on the bottom porch step as Lizzie opened the front door. She looked back at him. "I wish there was more that I could do for him. I feel so bad about this."

The urge to take her in his arms and comfort her was overpowering. He clenched his hands into fists at his sides to keep from reaching for her. "We are to take care of his sheep. That is all Joe wants from us. Get some rest, Lizzie. Tomorrow will be a long, busy day."

In the days to come, she would be working by his side. The joy the thought brought him was bittersweet. They would have a few days together, maybe a few weeks if she stayed through the lambing, but she wouldn't stay with him forever.

Carl wasn't surprised to see Lizzie just after dawn the next morning. He hadn't slept well and he doubted she had, either. She came down to the barn dressed in a faded green dress with her hair covered by a matching green kerchief instead of her usual black *kapp*. She carried a basket over one arm. When she drew near, he could see the puffiness in her eyes. She must have cried herself to sleep.

He longed to offer a comforting hug, but knew she wouldn't welcome such a gesture.

She held out the basket. "I have some cold biscuits and sausage with cheese and a thermos of coffee. It's not much."

"It's fine. I'm not that hungry."

"Neither am I."

"Save them for later."

She set the basket aside and pulled on a pair of her grandfather's work gloves. "I promise to do only what you tell me and exactly what you tell me. Where do I start?"

"You can start by not being so hard on yourself."

"I have put my grandfather in the hospital and made twice as much work for you. I'm not being hard on myself."

"Okay. First, we need the floor clean around where I'm working. You'll need to keep it raked and swept to prevent hay and other bits of debris from getting into the wool."

She grabbed a broom and began cleaning the old wooden floor of the barn with a vengeance.

Carl smiled at her eagerness. She was determined to be as much help as another man. He knew she felt badly about the accident, but she was going to wear herself out if she kept trying so hard. "Pace yourself, Lizzie. We have a lot more to do."

When they had the floors cleared, Carl brought in the rams that hadn't been shorn the day before. He wouldn't let Lizzie help until they were done and outside in their own separate enclosure.

He kicked the fleece aside and said, "Now we can move the first bunch of ewes into the catch pen. I'll need you to catch a sheep and bring her to me. When I pull her out and hold her, you need to squirt a dose of medicine into her mouth and then make note of it in our record book."

"I'll do whatever you need me to do."

She made a grab for the first animal and tried to pull it to where he stood. It was amusing to watch a one-hundred-and-twenty-pound girl trying to pull a two-hundred-pound animal with four splayed feet and a lot of determination across the pen. Finally, she gave up and the ewe scampered away from her.

Carl started to laugh until he caught sight of Lizzie's face. There were tears in her eyes. "I can't do any of this," she wailed.

"Sure you can. You just have to learn how to control sheep." He caught a ewe in the corner and said, "Come here. You place your hand firmly under her jaw and around her nose like this." He demonstrated. "Then you lift their nose up. This move will keep an ewe still if you press her against a wall or fence so she can't spin away."

Lizzie wiped her cheeks with the back of her hands. "So how do I get her to you?"

"You keep her nose up, put a hand on her hind end, and you walk her backward like this." He demonstrated moving the reluctant ewe to the shearing gate. "They won't all come easily, but most of them can be convinced this way."

He proceeded to give the sheep her medicine and then said, "Now I want you to hold this one here while I step out."

Lizzie looked dubious, but she did as he asked. The sheep, sensing a weaker hand, began to struggle, but Lizzie leaned into her, pushing her against the wall and holding her still.

"Good girl."

He stepped out of the shearing gate, grabbed the sheep from her, took it down to the ground and began to snip away. "While I'm cutting the fleece off, I want you to look up the ear-tag number in our flock record book and mark that she has been wormed. You'll see a place for a checkmark for the medication, a place to write a note if the animal needs a closer checkup because she's sick or acting strange."

"Okay." She flipped through the pages of the book and quickly made a note.

By the time she finished making the entry, he had the fleece off and allowed the ewe to regain her feet. Bleating loudly, she scampered down the runway and out into the corral beyond.

"Ready to bring me the next one?"

"Aren't you going to roll up the fleece?"

"I'll wait till we have a few piled here, and then we will clean and bag them."

From the group milling in the small pen, she grabbed the next one and moved it within Carl's reach. He pulled it from the pen and proceeded to shear it. In this way, they went through the morning. Sometimes, Lizzie managed to have one ready for him. Often, he had to step in and help her. By midmorning, he made the catch pen smaller so the sheep had less room to evade her.

At noon, Lizzie dusted off the front of her apron. She was breathing hard, but looked pleased at her accomplishments. "That was the last one."

"Twenty down, one hundred and ninety left to go."

Her eyes widened. "One hundred and ninety more?"

"Give or take. There will be a half dozen or so that we will cull, so they won't be sheared."

"What will we do with them?"

"I'll take them to the sale barn later this spring. Some will be purchased for slaughter, but a lot of them become fluffy lawn mowers. It's not a bad way for a sheep to live out its days. Come, I'll show you how we take care of the fleece."

He laid the first one from the pile on the table. "We pick off the really dirty wool and any grass or hay that might be stuck in it. Then we fold them up like this." He demonstrated and carried it to a gigantic plastic bag that was held upright by a large wooden frame with boards a few feet apart like a ladder on the sides of it.

"I've been wondering about this thing. It looks like a windmill without a top."

"The slats are so that I can climb up and get inside the plastic bag to tromp down the wool."

"That sounds like something I can do for you. It's got to be easier than wrestling sheep."

"It is easy, but, honestly, you don't weigh enough to pack down the fleece."

She looked for a second as if she wanted to argue with him but quickly thought better of it. "I'll fold the fleece, and you stuff the bag."

"It's a deal."

"Is it time for me to bring in more sheep?"

"It's time for a rest and some lunch. After that, I'll sharpen my shears, sweep off the platform and we'll start all over again."

She grimaced as she rubbed her hands together. "I had no idea their wool could be so greasy."

"It's lanolin. It gives you soft skin." He held out his hand. She ran her fingers across his palm. In a heartbeat, his mouth went dry. He inhaled sharply as his heart beat faster.

She must've sensed something, because her gaze locked with his. He wanted more than the brief touch of her fingers. He wanted to hold her hand. To reach out and pull her close. He wanted to learn everything there was to know about this amazing woman.

She quickly turned away. "I'd better get something ready for lunch. I hope cold sandwiches will be okay."

"That will be fine."

"Goot."

He watched her hurry away and wished he had a reason to call her back.

Lunch and the rest of the afternoon passed in an awkward silence. Carl tried to keep his mind on his work, but he was constantly aware of where she was and what she was doing. Her boundless energy began to lag in the late afternoon. He called a halt to the work even though he hadn't finished nearly as many animals as he had hoped to.

He went to clean up while Lizzie returned to the house. An hour later, he came in to find his supper waiting for him. Lizzie was seated in her usual place, but she was fast asleep, slumped over the table with her head pillowed on her arms.

Carefully, so that he wouldn't wake her, he picked up

his plate, meaning to take it outside. Instead, he found himself frozen in place watching her sleep.

He studied the wisps of wild red curls that wouldn't be contained beneath her scarf, the high cheekbones of her face, the way her eyebrows arched so beautifully. He had never seen a more lovely woman.

Once, he would have had the right to court her. To drive her home after a Sunday singing or to slip away with her after dark to attend a barn party or simply take a long walk in the woods. Once, but not now.

Such a thing was impossible. He had failed God with his weak faith. He should have died alongside his sister. He should have accepted the fate God willed for him and for one small girl and joined them in Heaven. Instead, his cowardice made him break his covenant with God.

Any future he might imagine with Lizzie was nothing but a wisp of smoke pouring from the barrel of a fired gun. A puff of white mist lost in the wind that could never be called back.

Lizzie squirmed into a more comfortable position and sighed deeply. He had no future with her, but he had this moment to remember all his days.

His food was cold by the time he let himself out the door. Duncan was lying on the porch waiting for him. The dog sat up. "Stay. Guard," Carl told him.

The big dog moved in front of the door and lay down. Knowing Duncan would alert him to any problems, Carl walked down the hill to his cold and dark hut.

A SERIES OF LOVE INSPIRED NOVELS!

GET 2 FREE BOOKS!

W

e'd like to send you **two free books** from the series you are enjoying now. Your two books have a combined cover price of over $10, but are yours to keep absolutely FREE! We'll even send you two wonderful surprise gifts. You can't lose!

Each of your FREE books is filled with joy, faith and traditional values as and women open their hearts to each other and join together on a spiritu journey.

FREE BONUS GIFTS!

*We'll send you two wonderful surprise gifts, worth about $10, **absolutely FREE**, just for giving our books a try! Don't miss out — MAIL THE REPLY CARD TODAY!*

Visit us at
www.ReaderService.com

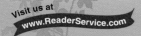

GET 2 FREE BOOKS!

HURRY!
Return this card today to get 2 FREE Books and 2 FREE Bonus Gifts!

YES! Please send me the **2 FREE books** and **2 FREE gifts** for which I qualify. I understand that I am under no obligation to purchase anything further, as explained on the back of this card.

PLACE FREE GIFTS SEAL HERE

❑ I prefer the regular-print edition
105/305 IDL GEAV

❑ I prefer the larger-print edition
122/322 IDL GEAV

FIRST NAME

LAST NAME

ADDRESS

APT.#

CITY

STATE/PROV.

ZIP/POSTAL CODE

Chapter Eight

For Lizzie, the following day started out much like the day before, except she ached from head to toe. There wasn't a muscle in her body that didn't hurt.

She wasn't used to such physical labor. She kept house for her uncle and sisters and did all the cooking, canning and most of the laundry. Twice a day she helped with the milking, but she didn't have to wrestle the Holsteins into their stanchions.

Sheep were stubborn, smelly and loud. She had no idea why her grandfather thought so much of them. But he did, and she would help Carl care for them until Joe was able to do so himself. For however long it took.

By midmorning, she was working some of the kinks out of her shoulder when she spotted a wagon turning into the drive. She looked at Carl. "Are you expecting someone?"

He finished clipping the ewe he had between his knees and then straightened to look out the barn door. "No, I'm not expecting anyone. Joe doesn't get visitors."

A buggy turned in behind the wagon. "I hope it's not the bishop's wife." Lizzie had no idea how to prevent the woman from entering Joe's house if she wanted to.

Together, she and Carl walked out of the barn. On the

front seat of the wagon, she recognized Adrian Lapp and his son, Kyle. Several young Amish men she didn't know jumped down from the wagon bed behind them.

The buggy pulled in with Katie Sutter and Sally Yoder on the front seat. They got out and began pulling large picnic hampers from the back.

Lizzie glanced at Carl. He just shrugged. "It looks like we've got some help."

Adrian and his young men approached them. Adrian said, "I've heard that your animals don't spit when you shear them. I thought I would come see this wonder for myself."

He gestured to a gray-haired man in blue jeans and a plaid shirt behind him. "This is Sheldon Kent. He's not Amish, but he says he knows how to get the wool off a sheep."

The man held up a pair of hand shears identical to the ones Carl used. "It's been a few years, but I reckon I still know my way around a fat woolly," he said in a thick Scottish brogue.

Carl broke into a wide smile. "Fat woollies I have aplenty. This way and thanks for the help."

Lizzie turned to Katie and Sally. "How did you know?"

"Faith Lapp told Bishop Zook about Joe's accident. He knew Sheldon Kent from over by Berlin and went to see if he could help shear. It's a blessing that Sheldon was free and could come. The bishop stopped by to tell us yesterday about his plan. We found a few more volunteers to help and here we are. Where would you like this food?"

"In the house, I guess. Is the bishop's wife coming?"

"Not today. Why?" Katie asked slowly.

"For some reason, Grandfather doesn't want her in the house."

Katie and Sally looked at each other and burst out laughing.

"What's so funny?" Lizzie asked.

Katie struggled to control her giggles. "Esther told my mother-in-law that she wouldn't set foot on Woolly Joe's property."

"The bishop's wife said that? I wonder what it's all about." Lizzie knew her grandfather wouldn't explain even if she asked him.

"We may never know. Grab that box off the back-seat, Lizzie. We'd best get ready to feed our men." Katie marched ahead into the house.

Sally waited until Lizzie extracted the box and then walked beside her to the house. "Tell me, have you found out anything about your grandfather's hired man?"

Lizzie looked at her sharply. "What do you mean?"

"He is something of a mystery around these parts. No one knows where he came from. He rarely speaks to anyone except the children. Some people think he's ex-Amish. Some people say he's a weird Englisch fellow that's soft in the head."

Lizzie bristled. "Carl is not soft in the head, but he was raised Amish."

"I'm sorry. I didn't mean to insult your friend."

"We're not friends. He lives and works here, that's all. He works hard, and he's a good shepherd. He cares about the sheep. My grandfather respects Carl's privacy and I do, too."

"You are right to do so. I was being nosy. Forgive me."

Lizzie realized she had spoken too harshly. "There's nothing to forgive. I'm tired and short-tempered today and worried about my grandfather."

Sally smiled. "Of course. I think a hot cup of tea is called for. Come in and rest."

* * *

With so much help, the shearing was finished by the end of the day. Carl thanked the men who had come. Joe would be happy to learn the job had been finished in record time. When the wagon finally rolled out of the yard in the late afternoon, Carl looked at Duncan sitting beside him. "This will give us a few more days to get ready for the lambing."

He knew how to do that, but he didn't know how to take care of a convalescing patient with a broken hip. Or a young woman who was so determined to make a place for her family.

Would Lizzie stay and help take care of her cantankerous grandfather, or would she move to the Sutters' farm as she had planned? It was something they should talk over. Perhaps now Joe could be convinced that he needed his granddaughters to come stay with him. Lizzie would be thrilled if they could all stay together.

Carl went to his hut and changed out of his grimy work clothes. Wrapping them and a few other items in his sheets, he carried them all to the back porch. It was his intention to do his own laundry, but Lizzie heard him filling the machine with water and came outside.

"I can do those for you, Carl."

"I can manage."

She took the box of laundry soap out of his hand. "You have been working all day, while I wasn't allowed to do anything harder than brew a pot of coffee."

"You've been working nonstop since you arrived. I think you deserve a few hours of rest."

"And now I've had them. Supper will be ready in a little while. I'm going to walk over to the telephone booth and call the hospital to check on my grandfather."

While the Amish did not allow telephones in their

homes, Carl knew that Joe's congregation allowed a shared telephone that was located centrally to several farms. "I'll walk over with you when you go."

Was he being too bold? Hadn't he convinced himself last night that he didn't deserve her interest? Even so, he held his breath and waited for her answer.

She smiled and nodded. "I would be glad of the company. *Danki*."

He grinned, giddy with relief. "I'm anxious to hear how he is doing, too."

The phone booth was a half mile from the end of the lane. To Carl's knowledge, Joe had never used it. Carl had used it only once. A year ago, he had called the Englisch bakery where his sister Jenna worked to let her know that he was okay. He knew she would relay his message to their parents. Jenna begged him to come home, but he couldn't face his family yet. Not until he believed he had earned God's forgiveness. In a moment of weakness, he gave Jenna his address.

She had been writing to him every week since that day. He had read the first two without answering them, but he couldn't bear to read them after that. It was too great a reminder of his shame and his loss.

He thought a lot about that phone call as he walked beside Lizzie. He missed his family just as Lizzie missed hers. Although he knew he might never see his home again, he wanted Lizzie to have the people she loved around her.

It had been a long time since he'd given a thought to what someone else needed. He said, "The doctor told Joe that he was going to need extra help when he came home."

"I've been thinking about that. I reckon I should tell Katie Sutter that I won't be able to work for her and that she should look for someone else."

"Actually, I was thinking that your sisters might be able to come help care for him."

She shook her head. "They don't have the money to get here. I sent all that I have, but it is only enough for one of them. I don't know if Clara will come without Greta and Betsy."

"Have you written to them about their grandfather?"

"I haven't. I don't know how to explain what a mess I've made of things here."

"Perhaps knowing that you need help taking care of him will convince Clara to come."

"I hadn't thought of that. You may be right."

"It happens sometimes."

She gave him a puzzled look. "What happens sometimes?"

"Sometimes it happens that I'm right. I was making a joke, Lizzie."

She pressed her hand to her mouth and giggled. It was the cutest sound he'd ever heard. They arrived at the phone booth all too soon for him.

He waited outside the door until she came out. "How is he?"

"The nurse said he is doing very well except for a small fever. She said he is cranky, and he's been complaining about the food."

"That doesn't surprise me. If he wasn't complaining about something, I'd be really worried."

"She said to expect him to stay there for a week or so depending on how well he does with his physical therapy."

"I almost wish they would keep him longer."

"Why?"

"Once the lambing season starts, I'm not going to have time to look after him. Knowing Joe, he's going to want to be out helping."

She sighed. "We must be thankful that he is recovering. If he allows me to stay, I will take care of him while you take care of the lambs."

"I hate to see you give up a paying job that means so much to you."

"It's my family that means a lot to me. Grandfather is part of my family even if he doesn't want to be. I'll stay until he's fit, and then I will find a job. Clara's wedding isn't until the first week of May. I have time yet to earn the money my sisters will need to join me."

"Knowing that you'll stay until Joe is mended takes a load off my mind."

She blushed and smiled sweetly. "I'm glad."

"What else did the nurse say?"

She updated Carl on what was said as they walked home. He tried to slow the pace to make the trip last longer, but Lizzie wasn't one to drag her feet. Was her haste because of the work she had yet to finish, or was it his presence that she was eager to escape?

He couldn't blame her if that was true. He didn't belong in the company of an Amish maid. Most Amish people would frown on even this harmless activity because of his exclusion from their faith. Those who didn't know that he had been placed in the Bann could criticize Lizzie for spending time alone with an outsider. Either way, he was putting Lizzie's reputation at risk. Today, the community had rallied around her. He wanted it to stay that way. The less time he spent with her, the better it would be for her.

He stopped walking. "I've got a ram out in the upper pasture that I need to check on. I noticed an abscess on his back when I sheared him."

She shot him a perplexed look. "But it's almost suppertime. Can't it wait until tomorrow?"

"I'm not hungry. Go ahead and eat without me. Don't

look for me tomorrow, either. I've got a lot of lambing pens to get set up."

"You have to eat, Carl."

"I've got food at my place. It's not as good as your cooking, but I'll make do."

"I'm not going to let you go a whole day without a hot meal and that's that."

"Okay, you can feed me supper tomorrow." He started backing away.

"Are you sure?" She sounded reluctant to see him go.

That was all the more reason for him to leave, but he couldn't believe how difficult it was to walk away. "I'm sure. Have a good night, Lizzie."

"*Guten nacht,* Carl."

He stopped a few feet away from her and turned back. "My place is only a quarter of a mile away if you need something."

She smiled softly. "I know."

"Right." He gestured toward the pasture. "I should get going."

"Be careful around those rams. I have no idea how to run a sheep farm."

If anyone could do it, she could. "I don't think it would take you long to learn."

Although Lizzie's thoughts and prayers frequently turned to her grandfather and to her sisters while she worked the next day, she was amazed at how often they strayed to Carl. A dozen times during the morning, she stopped what she was doing to look out the window in the hopes of catching a glimpse of him. Each time, she was disappointed.

Was he avoiding her, or did he really have so much work to do that he couldn't even stop in for a cup of coffee? She kept a pot warm on the stove just in case. In the early afternoon, she poured herself a cup, took one sip, grimaced and poured the rest down the drain. It was strong enough to float a horseshoe. She was glad that Carl hadn't had a chance to sample it.

She finally caught a glimpse of him and Duncan walking across the pasture toward his hut around six o'clock. She realized if she made another trip to the phone booth that their paths would pass close to each other in front of his home. That way, she could pretend she hadn't set out to meet him deliberately.

Quickly, she changed her stained apron for a clean one. She patted any stray hairs into place and went out the door, but she was doomed to disappointment. She didn't meet Carl or Duncan on her walk. Had Carl seen her coming his way and changed directions?

She continued along the path feeling let down and more disappointed than she should have been. When had she come to depend so heavily upon Carl's presence to cheer her?

Today, like yesterday, the sun shone brightly in the sky. The same flowers bloomed in the grass along the roadside and the trees pushed the same green leaves open. A lark sang a happy song from the fence off to one side. The sights, sounds and the smells of spring were still all around her, but they seemed muted without Carl's companionship.

The realization troubled her.

As soon as her grandfather was able to live on his own again, she would have to leave. She had grown far too fond of Carl in the short time that she'd known him. She couldn't delude herself into thinking otherwise. Wasn't she out here hoping that he would join her? Such feelings were a recipe for disaster, for both of them.

When she reached the phone booth, her call to the hospital only added to her worries. The nurse she spoke to seemed reluctant to share much information. She did relay the fact that Joe still had a fever and that he was undergoing more tests.

On the way back to the farmhouse, Lizzie picked up the mail. It was too soon to expect an answer from Mary, but Lizzie was disappointed anyway when there wasn't anything for her.

Her grandfather's newspaper was there. She wondered if the hospital would supply him with a copy. Tomorrow, when she called again, she would ask. She thumbed through the rest of the mail. There were a few pieces addressed to her grandfather and a letter for Carl that caught her attention.

She studied it briefly. Was it from the same person that had written to him last week? She hadn't paid attention to the previous letter, so she had no way of knowing. The return address on the one she held was Reedville, Pennsylvania. Was that where he was from? The sender's name was Jenna King.

A sister or his mother? A wife? The block printed letters of the address had a childlike quality. His child perhaps? He could be married with a half dozen *kinder* for all she knew. It was an unsettling thought. The envelope in her hand sparked far more questions than answers about the man. She was curious to see what Carl would do with this letter.

She didn't see him until she rang the bell for supper that evening. He came in and washed up without looking at her. Was he still upset with her for causing Joe's accident? She couldn't think of anything else she had done to make him avoid her.

Maybe he sensed her interest and wanted to stem it. She blushed at the thought.

"Have you heard anything about Joe?" he asked.

"I called the hospital again. They told me he was running a fever. I got the feeling the nurse wasn't telling me everything."

He leaned a hip against the counter as he dried his hands. "You think Joe is worse than they are letting on?"

"I don't know what to think."

"What did the nurse say?"

"That he is still running a fever and they are doing more tests."

"Maybe I should go see him."

"Would you? That would be wunderbar."

"If it will ease your mind, I'll see if I can get a ride with Samuel Carter tomorrow. He's a local English fellow who uses his van to drive Amish folks when they need to travel farther than a buggy can go."

She bit her lower lip, then said, "You must not do it as a favor to me."

"Right. No favors. Okay. It will ease *my* mind to see how he's doing firsthand."

"Goot." The small distinction seemed silly, but it relieved her conscience.

The sound of a car pulling up outside and Duncan's mad barking made them both glance outside. "Who is that?" she asked.

"I have no idea."

Lizzie opened the door and saw Dr. Zook get out of a dark blue car. He wasn't dressed in his white coat this evening. He was wearing a light gray sweater and a pair of faded blue jeans.

He nodded to her. "Good evening, Miss Barkman. I thought you might like an update on Joe's condition."

Lizzie stepped back from the door. "Of course. We were just talking about him. Please come in. Can I get you a cup of coffee? We were about to have supper. You are welcome to join us. Several of the local women have left desserts with us. I understand that Nettie Imhoff's peach pie is quite good."

"It is. I've had it on several occasions, but I don't need anything tonight, thank you. I can only stay for a few minutes. I wanted to let you know that your grandfather isn't getting along as well as I had hoped. Unfortunately, there have been some complications."

Lizzie pressed a hand to her heart as fear made it thud painfully. "What type of complications?"

"His blood work shows that he has an infection. We believe it's in the surgical site."

"Is it serious?" Carl asked from the kitchen.

The doctor turned to include Carl in the conversation. "It can be, but at this point it's not life-threatening. It is, however, something we need to keep a close eye on. What this means is that Joe will have to remain in the hospital for at least another week of IV antibiotics. I'm sorry. I know this is not what you want to hear."

No, Lizzie had been hoping to hear that Joe would be home soon and up and around in no time.

Carl held out his hand to the doctor. "We appreciate you stopping by in person to give us the news."

"It was on my way home from making rounds at the hospital. We'll let you know if there's any change in his condition. I also wanted to visit with you about his care when he does get to come home. He's not going to be able to live alone for at least six weeks."

"Six weeks?" Her heart sank at the news. It was only six weeks until Clara's wedding. She wouldn't be able to get a job and make enough to pay Greta and Betsy's way here.

"Will that be a problem?" Dr. Zook asked.

Lizzie raised her chin. "*Nee,* I'll be here for as long as he needs me."

"And I'll be close by," Carl added.

"I know the Amish take care of one another, but I've also heard that Joe is something of a recluse. The nurses at the hospital tell me he's turned away all his visitors, including the bishop."

"He can be cantankerous," Carl admitted.

"That's what worries me. I don't want him trying to do things by himself too soon."

"I'll see that he behaves. He'll listen to me." Carl's tone reassured Lizzie and the young doctor.

"Good. Joe's caseworker will come to visit with you about his needs before he comes home. If you have any questions, feel free to stop by my office or give me a call." With that, the young doctor nodded goodbye and went out the door.

Lizzie pressed a hand to her forehead. "Daadi has to be all right. I've only just gotten to know him again. I can't bear the thought of losing him."

Carl looked worried, too, but he said, "Joe is a tough old goat. He's going to be fine. We have to believe that."

He was trying to reassure her and she was grateful for his effort. "You're right. I'm borrowing trouble to worry about something I can't change. All things are in God's hands."

"I'm sorry that I can't do more to ease your worries." His tone was soft and filled with regret.

"I appreciate that." Lizzie looked away from the sympathy in his eyes. It was becoming much too easy to accept his kindness when she knew she shouldn't.

She indicated the packet of mail on the table. "Would you go through this and see what needs to be taken to Joe? There's a letter for you, too."

"Thanks." He picked up the bundle and leafed through it. He separated one letter, carried it to the stove and dropped it into the fire. She knew without asking that it was the one addressed to him.

It was none of her business what Carl did with his correspondences, but she was still shocked. Her curiosity about him rose tenfold. Who was the woman who wrote to him, and why did he burn her letters?

Chapter Nine

After a hectic week, Lizzie expected a day of rest on Sunday, since there was no church to attend. Amish congregations gathered for worship every other week. The "off" Sunday, when there was no preaching service, was reserved for quiet reflection, visiting and family time.

At home, it would have been the day for reading quietly or perhaps going to visit a friend or neighbor. Because she and her sisters didn't have the extended family so common among Amish communities, they seldom visited anyone but a few close neighbors. Her uncle wasn't a popular man. It was rare that anyone came to visit them.

The morning passed much as she expected, but a little before noon, Elam and Katie Sutter drove in. Sally Yoder sat in the back holding Jeremiah while Rachel leaned out the window with wide round eyes.

Glad for the distraction that would prevent her constant worry about her sisters, Lizzie went out to greet them. Three people emerged from the back of the buggy. As she was being introduced to Levi and Sarah Beachy and Naomi's daughter, Emma Troyer, several more buggies turned into the lane. Lizzie looked around for Carl, but he remained out of sight. The second buggy held the Lapp family, and the last vehicle belonged to a couple she hadn't met. Faith introduced them to her as Joann and Roman Weaver.

Joann, a plain woman with amazing green eyes, said, "I think I remember you. Didn't you go fishing with your grandfather when you were little?"

"Now that you mention it, I do remember going to a lake with him, but I remember throwing rocks into the water, not fishing. Are you the little girl who could skip stones so well?"

Joann laughed. "I don't know that I did it well, but I did it often, until I learned that it scared the fish away. I'm so happy to see you again. I feel like I have discovered a long-lost friend."

Her husband wore a sling on his left arm. "I believe you have. Just remember, I'm still your number-one fishing buddy."

"Like I could forget that." The smile the couple shared made Lizzie wish that someone would smile at her that way.

It was a silly thought. She never expected to be courted. She never wanted to be courted. So why would she long for such closeness with any man?

"Newlyweds," Sally whispered in Lizzie's ear as she walked past. "They only have eyes for each other."

The children ran past her and greeted Duncan. Then they immediately went down to the barn to look at the sheep. The next time Lizzie glanced their way, she saw Carl was with them. He was holding Rachel and letting her pet one of the ewes. She squealed each time she touched the animal's soft wool, making Carl laugh at her antics. Joann and Roman went down to visit with Carl. Were they friends of his? Did they know his history?

Sally bounced down the steps of the porch and stopped beside Lizzie. "Good, those two have gone to make sheep's eyes at the sheep instead of at each other. For two people who couldn't stand one another just a year ago, they certainly get along well now."

Lizzie watched Carl explaining something to Joann and wondered if there was someone in his past that he loved, or was loved by in return. Were the letters he burned from his mother or a sister? Or were they from a wife that he'd left behind? How many letters had he ignored? More important, why?

Katie soon claimed her attention, and Lizzie went inside to discover a lunch had been laid on her table with enough food to feed an army.

She passed an amazing day with her new friends. They laughed and told stories about each other and about her grandfather. They made Lizzie feel as if she had always been a part of their circle of friends.

Their closeness reminded her of her sisters. Katie was a lot like Clara. They were both quiet, deep thinkers. Greta, with her love of animals, would find a kindred spirit in Faith. Sally was only a little older than Betsy, but Lizzie could imagine them as friends and confidantes, boldly speaking their minds and giving the local boys a heartache or two.

If only she could get her sisters to Hope Springs, life would be so much better for all of them.

The afternoon passed quickly, and when the last of her visitors had gone, Lizzie walked out onto the porch and took a seat on one of the two green metal chairs along the side of the house. From the scuff marks in the railing's white paint, she suspected that both Carl and her grandfather spent evenings here with their feet propped up.

She had been sitting only a few minutes when she saw Carl leave the barn. He glanced in her direction. She raised a hand and waved. He hesitated, as if torn between coming to the house or going to his hut. Duncan had no difficulty making a decision. He loped across the yard and up the steps to sit between the chairs. Lizzie reached down to pet him. He licked her hand in doggy gratitude.

When she looked up, Carl was coming her way. He silently climbed the steps and took a seat. She almost giggled when he tipped his chair back and propped his feet on the rail in front of him. "You've had a busy day."

"I have been overwhelmed with visitors, that's true. You will be amazed at the amount of food that is on the table. They insisted on leaving everything. I may not have to cook for a month."

"That would be a shame. You're a mighty good cook."

She blushed at the compliment. "It seems that Grandfather has many friends. I had no idea. Do they visit often?"

"Not since I have been staying here, and that's almost four years now. Naomi Wadler comes a few times a year, but she never stays long. She keeps Joe's larder stocked with jars of garden produce, jam and fruit from her orchard and puts up the stuff he grows, too."

"Really? I wonder why. Are they related?" It was common practice for Amish families to care for their elders.

"Not that I know. I always thought she was sweet on him. I'm glad she does it or we would end up eating nothing but muttonchops and crackers."

"Sweet on my grandfather? Are you serious? He's old!"

Carl chuckled. "He may be old, but he can keep out of her way fast enough. She may be chasing, but he isn't ready to be caught."

"Naomi wasn't here today, but I met her daughter, Emma. I like her very much."

"I've never met her, but if she is anything like her mother, she is a formidable woman."

"I noticed you talking to Joann and Roman Weaver. Are they friends?"

"Don't you mean do they know I have been shunned?"

"*Nee,* I meant no such thing." Maybe she had been wondering that, but she wouldn't admit it now.

"Joann and Roman like to go fishing at Joe's lake. I speak to them now and again. A few times, they have left their catch with us. Joann is something of a bookworm. She was telling me today that llamas make good guard animals for sheep, plus, you can sell their fleece."

"Do they spit?"

He chuckled. "Worse than an alpaca."

"Let's stick with Duncan. He never spits." The dog wagged his tail at the mention of his name. She reached down and stroked his head.

"Is this what the off Sundays are like where you come from?" Carl asked.

"*Nee.* We seldom have visitors. Uncle Morris doesn't like it when our friends come over. He complains that we can't afford to feed everyone. What about you? What were Sunday afternoons like when you were growing up?"

"A lot like this. My mother has twelve brothers and sisters, and my father has five, so we were always inundated with cousins, aunts and uncles or we were traveling to visit them."

"You must miss that."

"Sometimes, but I like my privacy." He shot her a pointed look.

She ignored it. "Do you keep in contact with your family?"

"No."

"How sad. I thought perhaps the letters that came for you are from someone in your family. I saw the name on the return address was Jenna King. I know it's not my business…"

"You're right. It's not," he said abruptly.

She took offense at his attitude. "If you intend to be rude, I'm going inside."

He quickly stretched his hand toward her. "No, wait. Don't go yet. I'm sorry. It's just that I don't like to talk about my past."

"Talking helps, Carl."

"It can't change what has happened."

"No, but it can show us that we aren't alone in our troubles."

"In case you haven't noticed, Lizzie, I like being alone."

"In case *you* haven't noticed, Carl King, *you* don't." She rose and stomped into the house.

Duncan whined, sensing the tension that Carl tried hard to control. Lizzie enjoyed needling him. He reached out and ran his hand over the dog's silky head. "We used to like being alone, didn't we?"

Until Lizzie showed up and constantly made him aware of how barren his life was. Working, eating, sleeping and watching over the sheep had been satisfying enough for him until a week and a half ago. How could such a little slip of a woman turn things topsy-turvy in a matter of days?

Maybe he was drawn to her because she reminded him so much of Sophia. Like his youngest sister, Lizzie's enthusiasm sometimes outweighed her common sense. Still, he liked that about her. She saw what she wanted, and she worked to achieve it. But no matter how hard she worked at prying into his past, she was going to find herself up against a dead end. His crime was his own. He wouldn't share the story of how he fell so far from grace. He couldn't bear to see the look on Lizzie's face if she found out he had murdered someone.

The door opened and Lizzie came outside again. Her normally sweet expression was cold. She thrust a foil-wrapped plate into his hands. "Enjoy your supper…alone. I won't be cooking tonight."

She turned on her heel and marched back into the house. She didn't quite slam the door, but she shut it with conviction.

Duncan lifted his nose toward the plate. Carl held it out of his reach. "Oh, no, you don't." He raised his voice and shouted, "This is mine, Duncan, and I'm going to enjoy it alone!"

Somewhere in the house, a door slammed. Feeling slightly gratified at having had the last word, he walked down the hill toward his hut. At the door, he paused. As much as he hated to admit it, Lizzie was right.

There was a wooden chair outside his front door. He grabbed it and carried it toward the small creek that meandered through the pasture. He stopped beside an old stump that he could use for a table. From this vantage point, he could see the house up on the hill. Somehow, just knowing she was up there was a comfort.

He settled down to snack on cold fried chicken, carrot sticks and biscuits that were flaky and good, but they didn't measure up to Lizzie's. Not by a long shot.

The next day began with a flurry of work. Knowing that her grandfather would be unable to put in his garden or do such chores for several weeks, Lizzie attacked his garden plot with a vengeance. The weather had turned cold again. The taste of spring had been just that, a taste. March wasn't going to go out like a lamb.

It was nearly noon when she noticed Carl standing

outside the fence watching her. Finally, she couldn't bear his stoic silence any longer. She thrust her spade into the ground. "What are you staring at?"

"I have some composted manure and straw I need to get rid of. Shall I haul it over here? I don't want to do you any favors."

"Shall I go in the house so you can do it alone?"

He struggled to keep a grin off his face and lost. "I reckon I deserved that. I'm sorry I was cross with you yesterday."

"And I am sorry for being a nosy busybody. Your life is your own, Carl. It was wrong of me to pry. Can we be friends again? I really dislike eating alone."

"So do I, but can we be friends?"

She smiled. "I don't see why not. You are invaluable to my grandfather, and I wasn't joking when I said I didn't know how to run a sheep farm."

"You have been a good learner. Next year, you'll be able to wrestle the sheep to me with barely a thought. I may even teach you how to use the shears." He opened the garden gate and carried in a spade. He took a spot beside her and began to turn over the dirt.

"Next year. I hadn't thought that far ahead. I've been so focused on getting my sisters here. Will I even be here a year from now? So much depends on my family."

"Have you heard anything from them?"

Lizzie shook her head. "I only sent them my letter a week ago. I should hear something soon. I have another letter that I need to mail today. I had to explain how my foolishness has landed our grandfather in the hospital. I want them to be prepared for what they will find when they arrive."

"Did you tell them about me?"

"Only that you live on the property and you take care of the sheep."

He stopped digging to look at her. "Nothing else?"

"Nothing else."

He nodded and began to spade up the soil again. Working together, they finished half of the garden before Lizzie called a halt to the work. "I want to get my letter to the mailbox before the mail carrier goes by. We can finish the rest tomorrow."

Carl stepped on his spade, driving it deep into the earth. "I thought I would call the hospital and see how Joe is today."

"Let me get my letter and I'll walk with you part of the way. That is, if you don't mind?"

He chuckled. "I don't mind. Is there any coffee left from this morning?"

"I have tried keeping some on the back of the stove, but it just gets bitter. It won't take me long to make a fresh pot. You must tell me what vegetables Grandfather will want planted this spring."

"He's fond of kale and radishes, I know that. He likes cucumbers and the squash casserole Naomi brings over in the summer."

"I'll check with her for the recipe and see what variety of squash she uses." Lizzie walked through the garden gate ahead of Carl, happy to be on good terms once more.

The day became a pattern for the rest of the week. Over a cup of coffee in the midmorning, they discussed what work needed to be done and made plans to get as much done as they could before the lambs began to drop. Carl finished building the sheep pens while Lizzie continued to work on the garden until rainy weather put a stop to her outdoor activity. In the late afternoon or early evening, they would walk together to the phone booth. Normally,

Lizzie was the one who spoke to the nurses and relayed the information to Carl. Joe refused to take phone calls in his room. It was permitted by their church in such circumstances, but the hospital staff respected his wishes.

As the days passed, Lizzie began to worry that she hadn't heard from Mary or from any of her sisters. It was likely that Uncle Morris had forbidden them to contact her, but she hoped and prayed they would find a way. It was during those worry-filled times that Lizzie came to rely on Carl's words of reassurance.

It was strange that a man who had been shunned by others could be such a comfort to her. More than ever, she wanted to help him find his way back to the community that meant so much to each of them.

One evening, after hearing from the nurses at the hospital that Joe was doing better, Lizzie and Carl stopped at the mailbox on the way back to the house as had become their habit. Lizzie opened the front panel and pulled out the mail. Excitement sent her pulse racing when she saw an envelope with her name on it. She clutched it to her chest. "Finally! It's a letter from my friend Mary. Please, Lord, I hope she tells me that Clara is coming."

She handed Carl the rest of the mail and quickly tore open her letter. As she read, her excitement turned to shock.

She felt Carl's hand on her shoulder as her knees threatened to buckle. "Lizzie, what's wrong?"

She managed to focus on his face. "Mary writes that Uncle Morris was furious at my running away. He and Rufus have decided to push the wedding up. The banns were read at last Sunday's church service. The wedding will take place two weeks from today." Lizzie pressed a hand to her cheek.

"I'm so sorry. I don't know what to say."

Tears welled up in her eyes and trickled down her cheeks unheeded. He pulled his hand away. She missed his comforting touch immediately.

"What does Mary say about the money you sent? Clara may decide to come now that she knows how little time is left."

"She can't. Mary hasn't been able to see them or get my letters to them. Uncle Morris has forbidden her to visit. They don't know where I am or that I haven't abandoned them. Two weeks! I can't even return for the wedding. I sent all the money I had to help Clara leave. It was all for nothing. For nothing!"

She fled down the lane and rushed into the house, leaving Carl standing alone behind her.

Lizzie went through the motions of fixing a meal, cleaning the house and readying the garden for planting. The work kept her busy, but it couldn't take her mind off the fate of her sisters. She felt marooned in the ramshackle house with no hope of seeing them again. Even Carl's softly spoken words of reassurance and quiet strength couldn't lift her spirits.

She often felt his eyes on her. She tried to put on a brave front, but inside she was miserable. When she went to bed at night, she prayed fervently for the Lord's intervention and for the courage to accept her failure as His will.

Late one afternoon, she came in from feeding the chickens and saw an envelope on the kitchen table. She picked it up. Inside was several hundred dollars. For an instant, she thought her prayers had been answered, then she realized who had left the money.

It was the answer to her prayers, but it was one she couldn't accept.

Her hands trembled as she placed the envelope back on the table and turned away.

Carl was standing outside the screen door watching her. She realized in that moment how much she had come to care for him.

"You have not taken it from my hand," he said quietly.

"But I know it's from you."

"Your grandfather would say this way is acceptable."

"It is a wonderful gesture, but I can't take your money, Carl."

He pulled open the door and came in. "Tell me how to make it acceptable to you and I'll do it. It's all I have. Please, take it."

"I could not accept such a favor."

"Would you accept it from me if I had not been shunned?"

"But by your own admission you have been. I must hold true to the vows I spoke before God." Her grandfather once said shunning was a difficult and painful thing. Until this moment, she hadn't realized how right he was.

Carl's shoulders slumped in defeat. "You won't accept it even if it means never seeing your sisters again?"

"Even if it means that."

"You live your faith, Lizzie Barkman. God will surely smile on you."

"Just as He smiles on all His children," she said quietly.

Carl stared at the floor. "I could not hold true to my faith as you do. He has turned His face away from me."

She moved to stand in front of him. "That isn't true, Carl. God never turns away from us. It is we who turn away from Him. We give in to doubt and fear, but He knows our hearts. He knows we need His love. Forgiveness and acceptance are ours for the asking."

He shook his head. "I have asked for forgiveness many

times, but I have not received it. I don't know that I ever shall."

"If anyone knows you, they must surely see your goodness. Your desire to help me means more than I can say. I know now what my grandfather sees in you. You have such a generous heart."

He raised his eyes and stared at her for a long moment. "And you are a strong, brave woman."

"Not at the moment." She picked up the envelope and held it out to him. He took it from her and left the house. She sat down at the table and wept.

Chapter Ten

⟿

Lizzie stood by the mailbox waiting for the letter carrier to reach her. She spotted the white van stopped at a farm down the road and knew he would come her way next.

She couldn't let go of the hope that Mary would write and tell her something had changed. It had to change. Clara couldn't marry Rufus. It was unthinkable.

When the van pulled up beside her, she waited impatiently as the man in the gray uniform behind the wheel sorted through the stack in his hand. "Looks like only one today."

He held it toward her. "I haven't seen Joe for a couple of weeks. I hope he's okay."

She glanced at the letter and saw it was addressed to Carl. She put it in her pocket. "My grandfather is in the hospital with a broken hip."

"Man, that's tough. I'm sorry to hear that. My son and I were planning to stop in and buy a club lamb from him later this spring. Should we rethink that?"

"I'm afraid I don't know what a club lamb is, but Carl King is here. I'm sure he can help you."

"Great. A club lamb is one that's raised by a kid in 4-H or FFA, Future Farmers of America. Carl was the one who helped my son choose a lamb last year. It took second place at the county fair. My boy is hoping for first place this year."

"I'm sure Carl will be happy to help you again."

"He's really good with kids. My son learned more about how to take care of his lamb from Carl than he did from his 4-H leader. Well, give Joe my best." He nodded and drove away.

Lizzie started toward the phone booth next. Was it only two days ago that she strolled along this path with Carl at her side? It seemed as if a century had passed since then. So much had happened. So much had changed. Her mad scramble to get her sisters to Hope Springs had come to a painful stop.

As had her growing friendship with Carl.

Her refusal of his gift put his shunning front and center between them. As it should have been all along, she acknowledged.

Leaving the security and close-knit circle of her family had put her adrift in a sea of change. Nothing was as she imagined it would be. Nothing worked out as she had hoped. Carl's quiet, reserved strength had offered her shelter from the storm of events taking place around her. It was no wonder she grew to cherish his friendship so quickly.

He was a good man. She didn't doubt that, but he no longer believed as she did and that was unacceptable. He knew it, because he had stopped coming by the house. She had seen him out and about on the farm, but he didn't come in for coffee in the morning or for lunch, or for supper, for that matter.

In short, he left her alone.

And she missed him terribly.

She reached the phone booth and saw Duncan lying outside it. Her traitorous heart gave a happy leap before she could put her hard-won resolve into place. A few moments later, Carl emerged. He stopped short at the sight of her.

"*Gutenowed,* Carl." She was pleased that her voice sounded composed with just the right touch of reserve.

"Good evening." He looked haggard and worn, as if he hadn't been sleeping well.

"Were you checking on Joe?" she asked.

He hitched his thumb over his shoulder toward the phone. "Yes. He's doing much better today. He's been up walking with a walker. There's no sign of fever. Looks like the antibiotics have done the trick."

"That's wonderful news."

He shifted uncomfortably. "It is. He should be home in a week. Look, I've got to go. Are you doing okay?"

"I'm fine, and you?"

"I'm managing. Have a nice night." He tipped his hat and walked past her.

She watched him until he disappeared around a bend in the path that led to his hut. He never looked back. She wanted to call out to him, but she couldn't think of a reason to do so. She didn't want him to know how much she missed having him around.

Should she have taken the money he offered? It would have been enough, more than enough. She could have taken it, confessed later to the bishop and accepted his forgiveness. There were ways around the rules, but they weren't just rules to her. They were the glue that bound her Christian community together against the forces that would break it down, both from the outside and from within.

Because of the Ordnung, every Amish man and woman knew what was expected of them. They knew their purpose in life. The rules of their society weren't made to be broken or ignored. They were made to guide and to guard against the disruptions of the world that could come between the faithful and God. Accepting the Amish faith came at a great price. It was never done lightly.

She might regret not using Carl's gift, but she knew she had done the right thing.

If only she had her own money or something she could sell, but she owned nothing of value. She had little more than the clothes on her back. Her heart ached as she thought about the life Clara would be forced to live with an abusive husband.

It would be their mother's life all over again.

Lizzie remembered all too well the desperate attempts to keep peace in the house, waiting in agony for the simple spark that would set their father's temper ablaze. He was always sorry afterward, but his repentant behavior never lasted, yet their mother forgave him time and again.

Lizzie shuddered at the memories. Clara deserved better.

Lizzie was lost in her thoughts and didn't realize a buggy had stopped on the roadway until someone called her name. Sally Yoder waved and beckoned Lizzie to her side. Lizzie didn't recognize the woman seated beside her. She wore dark glasses and looked to be several years older than Sally.

"I'm so glad we ran into you. We were just on our way to a quilting bee at my cousin's house. Have you met Rebecca yet?" Sally asked.

Lizzie shook her head. "I don't believe so."

The woman in the dark glasses leaned around Sally. "Hi, I'm Rebecca Troyer. It's a pleasure to meet you, Lizzie. Everyone has been talking about the sudden appearance of Woolly Joe's relative. Almost no one knew he had a family. How is he doing?"

"He's better. He may be home in a week."

Sally smiled in relief. "That's wonderful news. The reason I wanted to see you was to ask if you would like to ride with my family to the church service on Sunday."

"That's very thoughtful of you, Sally. That would be great as long as it's not out of your way."

"Not at all. We will go right past your lane. How are you doing living by yourself out here?"

"It's very quiet, but there's no one to interrupt my work during the day. Grandfather's house is getting the scrubbing it deserves. I found some half-empty paint cans on the back porch, so I plan to spruce up the kitchen."

"That sounds like a monumental task. Are you free this afternoon? Would you like to come to the quilting bee with us? We are making a quilt for my aunt's fiftieth birthday."

"We would love to have you join us," Rebecca added.

"I'm afraid I have limited skill with a needle. Rebecca, did I see one of your quilts for sale at the inn in Hope Springs?"

"Yes, my Lone Star quilt. Naomi sold it yesterday. I'm always amazed when someone buys one."

"You shouldn't be," Sally said. "You have a wonderful talent. People recognize the value of your work. We should get going. Lizzie, we'll pick you up at eight o'clock on Sunday morning."

"I look forward to it." Lizzie waved as they drove away, but her mind was already reeling. She did own something of value. Something of enormous value to her, but was it valuable enough to buy one-way bus tickets for three young women from Indiana to Hope Springs?

She had her mother's beautiful wedding-ring quilt.

The very idea of parting with the only thing she had to remember her mother by was painful to contemplate. What if she sold it and her sisters still didn't come? Then she would have less than nothing.

She walked the rest of the way home and wrestled with her choices. She could break down and use Carl's money, sell her mother's quilt or accept that she could do nothing. None of them were good choices, but there was only one she could live with.

When she entered the house, she was surprised to see Carl in the kitchen with a box of oatmeal in his hand. He gave her a sheepish look and set it on the counter, like a little boy caught with his hand in the cookie jar. "I'm out of oatmeal. I knew Joe had an extra box. Do you mind if I use it?"

"Is that what you've been living on?"

He stuffed his hands in his front pockets. "I like oatmeal."

"So do I, but not for three meals a day. I'm having chicken and dumplings for supper. There's plenty. You're welcome to have some."

He hesitated, glanced at the oatmeal box, then said, "Thanks. Don't mind if I do."

She turned aside to hide the surge of happiness that engulfed her.

It was just supper. She had to make sure she didn't let her emotions get out of hand again. "I may have discovered a way to earn the money I need to send for my sisters."

"Have you found another job? I can manage without you until Joe comes home."

"*Nee,* I saw Sally Yoder and Rebecca Troyer a little bit ago. They were on their way to a quilting bee. It reminded me that Naomi sells quilts for local women at the inn. She sold one of Rebecca's recently. I have a wedding-ring quilt. I thought I would take it to her and see if she could sell it for me."

She busied herself putting plates on the table and

avoided looking at him. She didn't want him to see how hard her decision had been.

He was a difficult man to fool. "A wedding-ring quilt is often a part of a young woman's hope chest."

"I don't plan to marry, so I have no need of the quilt." She tried to sound offhand but failed miserably.

"I thought marriage was the goal of every young Amish woman."

She turned to face him and wrapped her arms tightly across her middle. "It's not the goal of this Amish girl. Every family needs a maiden aunt to help care for the elderly and to help look after the children. That's the life I want."

"I can't see you living a life without love in it. What has given you a distaste for marriage?"

"I didn't say I have a distaste for it. I just said it's not the life I want." She stuffed her hands in the pockets of her apron and encountered the letter she'd forgotten to give him.

She held it out. "This came for you. I'm sorry I didn't remember sooner."

He took it from her, stared at it for a long moment, then put it in his shirt pocket. At least he didn't toss it in the fire this time. Was that a good sign?

She finished putting supper on the table and they ate in silence. She was afraid he would resume his questions regarding her feelings about marriage, but he didn't. It was fully dark by the time supper was over. Low clouds had moved in, bringing with them a chilly wind.

Carl put on his cowboy hat and coat and took a lantern from a hook by the door. He raised the glass and used a match to light the wick. "I have one ewe out in the hilltop pen that I need to check on. I may have to move her into the barn if she isn't better by morning."

"All right. Is there anything I can do?"

"No, I'm just letting you know so you don't worry if you see a light out in the field. Good night, Lizzie."

"*Guten nacht,* Carl," she said and watched him go out. She carried the dirty plates to the sink and glanced out the window. Carl had stopped at the corral gate. He set his lantern on the fence post and took something out of his pocket. Was he going to read his letter? She held her breath.

He brought the envelope to the top of the lantern chimney. After a few seconds, it caught fire. He held it between his fingers, turning it slightly to keep from being burned until there was only a tiny bit left. He dropped the piece to the ground and watched until the fire consumed all of it. Then he picked up the lantern and walked out into the field.

Lizzie turned away from the window. Her heart ached for Carl and for the woman who wrote him every week. How she must love him to keep writing in the face of his continued silence.

Who was she?

It wasn't his intention to take supper with Lizzie when he went to the house earlier. He really did need the oatmeal. Even a large box didn't last long when a man ate it three times a day. Cereal was his only reason for being in her kitchen.

At least, that was what he told himself as he crossed the dark pasture with a lantern in his hand. He might have been able to convince himself of that fact if he had actually taken the oatmeal with him when he walked out.

It was still sitting on the counter where he'd left it. He was hungry, but not for food. He craved Lizzie's company. He longed for a glimpse of her smile, to see her look upon him with kindness and maybe something more.

Duncan came out of the dark to walk beside him. He glanced at the dog. "I'm a fool, you know."

Duncan's only response was to lope away.

"So much for venting my troubles to a friend." Carl walked on. The dog couldn't help him with his dilemma. It was something he would need to come to grips with on his own. Although he had only known Lizzie Barkman for two weeks, he was falling for her in a big way.

He'd tried staying away from her, but his efforts had been futile. He was drawn to her in a way that had nothing to do with a home-cooked meal and everything to do with the way she made him feel when she smiled. He was drawn to the warmth of her soul.

He hadn't questioned the wisdom of staying in Hope Springs since the day Joe offered him a place to live. Until she showed up, the farm had been a sanctuary for him. A place where he could retreat from the world and the harm he'd caused. Only, now his self-imposed solitude had abruptly lost its appeal.

Lizzie's rejection of his offer to help hurt deeply even though he had half expected what her reaction would be. It was his inability to help that hurt the most. It kept him awake at night and made him realize how truly separated he had become from those of his faith.

As it turned out, she didn't need his help. She'd found a way without breaking her promise of faith.

He stopped walking and looked back at the house. The light from the kitchen window went out. He watched as the faint light of her lamp passed through the living room and vanished briefly before it reappeared in the window of her second-story bedroom. Would she sleep beneath her wedding-ring quilt tonight? He recognized the distress she tried to hide when she talked about selling it. The decision hadn't been an easy one for her.

He watched her window until the light went out. It was one thing to be alone when it was his choice. It was another thing when he ached with the need to comfort Lizzie but could only watch her struggles from afar.

A new thought occurred to Carl as he stood beneath the brilliant stars strewn across the night sky. Was Lizzie's arrival the way the Lord had chosen to call him back to the faith he'd grown up in?

The next morning, Lizzie finished her chores and left a note for Carl telling him she had gone into town. After that, she climbed the stairs to her small bedroom and stared at the quilt on her bed. It was all she had to remind her of her mother. It was the only thing of value she owned in the world.

She pulled it off the bed and wrapped it around her shoulders. It wasn't the same as being hugged by her mother, but it was as close as she could come until they met again in Heaven.

Tears filled her eyes. She would never feel her mother's arms again, but she could have her sisters' embraces to comfort her. She would have to sell her heirloom to make that happen. In her heart, she knew her mother would understand.

Laying the quilt on the bed again, she folded it carefully. Then she placed it in the box and tied it shut with a length of string. With it tucked firmly under her arm, she walked down the stairs and out the door with a purposeful stride.

It took her over an hour to reach Hope Springs. At the door of the Wadler Inn, she hesitated. She took a moment to gather her courage, then she opened the door and walked in.

Naomi Wadler wasn't behind the desk. An elderly Englisch gentleman greeted Lizzie. "Good morning. How may I help you?"

Lizzie laid her box on the counter. "I have a quilt that I would like Naomi to sell for me."

Naomi appeared in the doorway of a small office behind the counter. "Did I hear my name? Lizzie, how nice to see you again. How is Joe getting along? We have all been praying for him."

"The doctor told us that he developed an infection, but he has improved with the antibiotics they are giving him. He could come home in a week, but he'll still need care and physical therapy."

"I'm glad to hear that. What can I do for you, child?"

"I have a quilt I would like you to sell for me."

"Is this it?" She motioned toward the box.

"*Ja,* it's not a new quilt." Lizzie broke the string and opened the box. She pulled out the quilt and tears stung her eyes again at the sight of the intricately pieced fabrics in muted blues, pinks and soft greens.

"This is lovely. Was it all done by one person? My buyers prefer quilts done by a single hand rather than the ones done at a quilting bee."

"My mother made it by herself. It's very dear to me, but I have no idea what it is worth to someone else."

Naomi's eyes softened. "Are you sure you want to sell it?"

"I don't want to, but I must." Lizzie choked back tears. "It's the only way I can afford to pay for my sisters to move here. It is desperately important that they come. I know my mother would understand and approve. That makes selling it a little easier."

Naomi came around the counter and slipped an arm across Lizzie shoulders. "Surely your grandfather would loan you the money."

"I can't ask him now. He has hospital and doctor bills to pay. His accident was my fault. Besides, you know what a recluse he is. He doesn't want us here."

"Doesn't want you here? You must be mistaken."

"I wish I were. I left my home and traveled here with the hope that my grandfather would take us in. Things have become very…difficult at home. He refuses to help."

"I thought Joe would do anything for Abigail's children."

"I know he is old and set in his ways. A house full of women would be disruptive for him. I try to understand and forgive him. Can you sell the quilt for me?"

Naomi smiled sadly. "Absolutely. I know someone who might treasure this as you would."

Lizzie stroked the quilt one last time. "*Danki.* I hope it will be useful to them. Do you know how soon I could expect it to sell?"

"A quilt of this quality will be snatched up in no time. Don't worry about that. I'll send my son-in-law out to the farm with the money for you as soon as I can. Take heart, Lizzie. Something good will come of this, you'll see. Our Lord is watching over you and your sisters."

Lizzie nodded. If only she could be sure this was the path He wanted them to travel.

Naomi began folding the quilt, but her sharp eyes were fixed on Lizzie's face. "Tell me, how are you getting along with Carl King? He's an interesting young man, isn't he?"

Chapter Eleven

Lizzie hoped she wasn't blushing as she looked away from Naomi Wadler's pointed gaze. "I think Carl is doing well enough. Frankly, I don't know what my grandfather would do without him. He's been a tremendous help with all the farmwork. I know that grandfather trusts him to take care of the place and everything on it," she added with a rush, all the while wondering if she had given away too much of her own feelings about Carl.

"I was more interested in how you are getting along with Carl."

"Me? I have barely seen him the past few days. He has a lot to do to get ready for the arrival of our lambs." It wasn't a lie. Carl had been making himself scarce. She didn't need to explain why.

"I've always liked that young man. It is a pity he no longer follows our Amish ways. I know that Joe is terribly fond of him."

Naomi was one of the few people that had visited the farm with any frequency. Lizzie couldn't pass up the opportunity to see if she knew something about Carl's past. "Grandfather told me a little about how they met. Did he ever tell you?"

It was Naomi's turn to look uncomfortable with the conversation. "Joe and I don't really talk a lot when I visit. Even when Abigail lived at home, Joe wasn't one to make idle chitchat."

"You mentioned you were a friend of my mother's. I would love to hear about her when she was young."

Naomi spoke to the gentleman behind the desk. "Charles, Miss Barkman and I will be in the café if you need me." She handed him the box with Lizzie's quilt. "Put this in my office, please."

Naomi came around the counter and hooked her arm through Lizzie's. "Let me treat you to some of the best shoofly pie you've ever had. My daughter makes it. I can tell you so many funny things about your mother."

Lizzie smiled at her. "What was she like when you knew her?"

"She came to live with us when she was only two and I was fifteen. I became her little mother. Did she ever tell you that I was the one who chipped her front tooth with a baseball bat when we were playing ball? Of course, it was an accident, but I felt so terrible about it every time I saw her smile."

"She never told us that." Lizzie allowed Naomi to lead her through a set of French doors to the Shoofly Pie Café that adjoined the inn.

Carl peeked in through the front window of the Wadler Inn. He didn't see Lizzie inside. He'd waited more than an hour after she left home to come into town, as well. He was sure she would have come straight here. He didn't want her to know what he had planned, but he was determined to help her reunite with her sisters.

When he stepped inside the lobby, the elderly Englisch

gentleman behind the counter smiled brightly. "Welcome to the Wadler Inn. How may I help you?"

"I understand that you have quilts for sale."

"Yes, we certainly do. You will find our area quilters are some of the very finest. Their creations are true works of art, although the Amish do not view them as such. The ones around the fireplace are the only ones we have at the moment, but more come in all the time."

"I'm actually interested in a wedding-ring quilt that was brought in this morning."

The man looked perplexed for a moment and then said, "Let me get Mrs. Wadler to help you. That quilt is not on display."

Carl relaxed. It hadn't been put on display, so it must be still available. The man went into the café next door and returned a few moments later with Naomi. Her eyes widened in surprise. "Why, Carl, what are you doing here? Joe is doing okay, isn't he?"

"As far as I know, Joe is being his cantankerous self with the hospital staff who get paid to put up with him. I'm here to buy a quilt."

Naomi's eyebrows inched higher. She glanced over her shoulder into the café and then back to him. "Did you have something special in mind?"

"It's a wedding-ring quilt."

She steered him toward the fireplace. She took a seat and he sat across from her on a plush sofa. "Do you know who made it?" she asked.

"I'm not sure who's stitched it, but Lizzie Barkman, Joe's granddaughter, would have been the one who brought it in."

"I see. It's a shame you didn't buy it from her before she left the farm this morning. It would have saved you both a lot of time."

He was going to have to admit why he was here. "I don't want Lizzie to know that I'm the one buying it."

"Why not?"

There was no way he was going to reveal his entire reason, but he said, "I know it means a lot to her, and I don't want her to feel beholden to me."

"I can understand that, but I'm sorry to tell you the quilt is no longer available."

"Do you mean you sold it already?"

She kept her gaze on the door to the café. He wondered if he had interrupted her lunch. "I haven't actually sold it, but I am holding the quilt for someone. If they choose not to purchase it, I will be sure and let you know."

He rubbed his palms on his thighs. "Lizzie has an urgent need for the money the quilt will bring. Please, let me know as soon as possible."

"By Monday. I will let you know by Monday. And now I must get back to my guest." She rose to her feet and he did the same.

"Thanks for your help." He had done all he could. One way or the other, Lizzie would get the money she needed.

Naomi tipped her head slightly to one side as she stared at him. "Joe has placed a lot of faith in you, Carl. Please don't let him down."

"Don't worry. His sheep are safe with me."

"I wasn't actually thinking about the sheep."

He was too stunned to reply. She gave him a wink and walked to the desk. "Charles, would you please arrange a driver for me on Sunday evening?"

"Yes, ma'am."

She waved to Carl. "I'll be in touch."

Sally and her family picked up Lizzie on Sunday morning and they joined the long line of buggies traveling single file along the country road. The line moved only as fast as the slowest horse. No one would dream of passing a fellow church member on the way to services. Such a move would be seen as rude and prideful. Even the young men with their high-stepping horses and topless courting buggies held to a sedate pace.

Lizzie found her gaze drawn to Carl's front door when they drove by the pasture gate. The door was closed. There was no sign of him. No smoke came from the chimney even though the morning was crisp.

Surely he must miss being part of a community that made God the center of their lives. Lizzie knew that she couldn't live cut off from her faith. She prayed that she never had to find out how it felt.

Like the previous prayer service, Lizzie was captivated by the simple but eloquent sermon delivered by Bishop Zook. He had a rare gift for preaching the word of God.

About an hour into the service, she noticed Katie Sutter was having trouble managing Jeremiah and the new baby. Both of them were fussing. Katie got to her feet and came to the back of the room where a set of stairs led to the upper level. When Jeremiah saw Lizzie, he reached for her and began hollering at the top of his lungs. Lizzie immediately got up from her seat and took charge of him.

"Bless you," Katie whispered. "I think he needs changing, and the baby wants to eat."

Lizzie wrinkled her nose. "He does." She followed Katie upstairs to one of the bedrooms. After she changed Jeremiah's diaper, she took him to the window to entertain him while Katie nursed his baby brother.

She pointed to a cardinal in the branches of the tree. "See the bird? Can you say *bird?*"

He babbled happily, but none of his words sounded the least like *bird.* He pointed a chubby finger at something and jabbered louder. Lizzie looked to where he was pointing and saw a dog. She realized it was Duncan. He was lying under the last buggy parked at the end of the row.

Lizzie leaned closer to the window. Was that Carl standing at the rear of the buggy?

It was. She straightened. What was he doing here? When the next hymn began in the room beneath her, she realized that Carl was singing, too. She couldn't hear him, but she could see the rise and fall of his chest and the movement of his lips.

She pressed a hand to her heart as pity welled up in her. How often had he stood apart from the worshippers and worshipped from afar? How sad that he wouldn't allow himself to return to what he clearly loved. More than ever, she wanted to find out what had driven him away.

Naomi softly opened the door to Joe's hospital room. The blinds were drawn. The room was dark. He was sitting up in bed, but he had fallen asleep with the newspaper spread over his chest. He wore a hospital gown. It was the first time she had ever seen him in something other than his blue work shirt or his black Sunday coat. He looked... helpless and alone.

The sight only strengthened her resolve. She walked to the side of the bed and took a seat in the single chair beside him. He slowly opened his eyes and focused on her. For a second, she thought she saw a glimmer of happiness before he frowned. He yanked the bedspread up to his chin. The newspaper went flying. "What are you doing here?"

"I came to see you."

"I'm not in the mood for company."

"That's hardly surprising. You haven't been in the mood for company for the past twenty years."

She laid the package she carried on his lap. "I brought you something."

He looked at it as if it might contain a snake. She almost laughed. It would be funny if it weren't so sad. "Go ahead, open it."

"You have no call to bring me presents."

"I declare, you can make a mountain out of a molehill faster than anyone I've ever met. Just open the package."

"I always knew you were a bossy woman."

"And I have always known that you are a stubborn man."

He lifted the lid of the box and gazed at the fabric with a perplexed expression on his face. "I don't have need of a quilt, but thank you. The stitching is quite fine."

"Abigail made it."

That shocked him. "Abigail? You don't mean my Abigail?"

"Yes, Lizzie brought it to the inn. She wants me to sell it. It's the only thing she has to remember her mother by. Abigail made a quilt for each of her daughters before she passed away. Lizzie was in tears when she handed it over."

Joe ran a hand lovingly over the fabric. "My Abigail always had a fine hand with a needle. You taught her well."

They both fell silent as thoughts of a shared past overwhelmed them. Naomi drew a deep breath. "She also had a stubborn streak. I suspect she got it from you."

"Why would Lizzie sell this?"

"Because she is desperate to bring her sisters here. Joe, we are old friends. What is Lizzie so afraid of?"

"Morris is making Clara marry a man that Lizzie feels is unsuitable. Harsh, even. That's why she came to Hope Springs. She was hoping I would take them in."

"And why have you turned your back on them? The

truth, Joseph," she demanded when she saw the belligerent glint in his eyes.

His expression slowly softened. "Lizzie is so much like her."

"But she is not Abigail. I know your daughter broke your heart when she married that man. She broke my heart, too. I saw what he was long before she would admit it. But hearts mend, Joe. Love mends a broken heart."

"I haven't any love left in me."

"You can't fool me, you old goat. Your heart is full of love for that young man you've taken in and for Abigail's daughter. You're just afraid to admit it. You're afraid of being hurt again."

"What if I took them in and they turned against me the way she did? I couldn't bear it."

"So you think it's better not to care at all? That's selfish. Has trying not to care for Lizzie made you happy, Joseph? The truth, now!"

"*Nee,* it has not."

"Then I see that you have two choices. Risk loving that wonderful child and her sisters and enjoy the best of what God has given you, or turn your back on His gift and keep on being a miserable shell of a man. What's it going to be, Joseph Shetler?"

"You shouldn't speak harshly to me, woman. I'm a sick man."

She leaned forward and laid a hand on his cheek. "Not so sick that you can't see how much I care for you, I hope."

He looked away. "I don't know what you're talking about."

"I had such a crush on you when I was young."

"A *maedel*'s foolishness. I'm almost twenty years older than you."

"Fifteen years. And while that was a lot when I was eighteen, it's not so much now that I'm sixty."

"You've gone soft in the head or something to be talking like this. You married a good man. The right man."

"Yes, I did, and I loved him dearly, but he's been gone for eight years now. Did you really think I brought all those canned vegetables and preserves to you out of Christian duty for the past five years?"

"Well...*ja,* I did."

"You silly man. I was trying to get your attention. I see now that the only way to accomplish that is by plain speaking. I'm right fond of you, Joseph Shetler. I would know now if you feel the same way."

"You can't expect a man to answer a question like that when he's under the influence of Englisch pain medicine."

"When I heard you had been taken to the hospital, I realized what a fool I have been to stay silent for so long hoping that you would speak first."

"You could have your pick of upstanding fellows. There's no reason for you to chase after a rickety old sheepherder. I can't even walk. What kind of husband would I be? Besides, a sheep farm is no place for a woman."

"Nonsense. So Evelyn hated sheep. So what? I like sheep. And I happen to like rickety old shepherds. Are you going to make me ask the question?"

He scooted up uncomfortably in bed and smoothed the spread over his chest. "What question would that be?"

She shook her head and began to gather up her things. "I reckon I'm a foolish old woman who thought that maybe, just maybe, I could have a second chance to love a man and be loved in return. I see I was wrong. Good night to you, Joseph. May the Lord bless and keep you." She rose and headed for the door.

"Wait," he called out.

She kept her gaze fixed on the doorknob. "I have been waiting, Joseph. I'm not going to wait anymore."

"All right, all right, have it your way."

Joy surged through her. She turned slowly to face him. "What does that mean exactly?"

"I'm not going to come courting in some fancy buggy."

"I don't need a fancy buggy."

"Well…it'll be lambing season soon. Any plans you've got will have to wait until summer."

She smiled broadly, walked back to his side and took his hand. "A quiet little summer wedding sounds wunderbar."

Worry filled his eyes. "Are you certain about this, Naomi?"

She bent down and kissed him. Then she whispered in his ear, "I've never been more certain of anything."

"I think I'm too old to be this happy." He wiped a tear from the corner of his eye.

"The good Lord didn't put an age limit on happiness, darling. Will you buy Abigail's quilt? If not, I will put it up for sale in my shop."

He looked down at the soft fabric. "I wish I knew what my daughter would want me to do."

Lizzie was raking up the previous year's litter from the vegetable garden when she saw a buggy coming up the lane on Monday. She didn't recognize the man driving, but she walked out to meet him. He drew up beside her and tipped his hat. *"Guder mariye."*

"Good morning and welcome."

"Are you Lizzie Barkman?"

"I am."

"I'm Adam Troyer. Naomi Wadler is my mother-in-law. She wanted me to deliver this to you." He leaned forward and held out an envelope.

"What is it?"

"I believe it is payment for your quilt."

"My quilt has been sold already? I only left it there on Saturday."

"I'm afraid I don't know the details, but it must've sold."

Lizzie opened the envelope. She looked up at Adam in shock. "This can't be right. There's far too much money here."

"Many of the quilts we sell fetch fine prices. The Englisch don't seem to care what they have to pay. I've seen some of the larger quilts at auction go for thousands of dollars."

Overwhelmed with gratitude and excitement, Lizzie realized she had more than enough to buy bus tickets for all her sisters.

"*Danki.* Please tell Naomi that I am eternally grateful for her help. Now I have to get this in the mail." As Adam turned the buggy around, Lizzie sprinted toward the house.

There is still time. There is still time. The refrain echoed in her mind.

"Carl! Carl, where are you?" She knew he had gone to town earlier, but she had seen him return. She wanted to share her joy and she wanted to share it with him. She raced up the steps, yanked open the screen door and ran full tilt into him.

Carl wrapped his arms around Lizzie to keep her from falling as they both struggled to catch their balance. Fear clutched at his heart. "What is it? What's wrong?"

She looked up, grinning from ear to ear. She patted his chest with both hands. "Nothing's wrong. Everything's right and God is good."

She didn't seem to notice that he was holding her. He noticed. She was close enough for him to see the flecks of gold in her bright hazel eyes. She was close enough to kiss. More than his next breath, he wanted to taste the soft sweetness of her lips.

Duncan nosed open the screen door and joined in with exuberance. He jumped up and planted his front feet on Lizzie's side, barking wildly. Carl slowly lowered his arms and reluctantly released her.

She turned her beautiful smile on the dog. "Yes, everything is fine, and you, Duncan, are a *goot, goot hund.*"

She took hold of his front feet and turned in a circle as the dog hopped to keep up with her. Laughing, she grabbed his face and ruffled his fur. Duncan dropped back to all fours, but continued to wag his tail as he fixed his eyes on her.

Carl folded his arms over his chest and tried not to be jealous of a dog. "Have you had good news about Joe?"

"I haven't heard anything about Grandfather today, but my quilt has been sold. I have money, Carl. Enough money to bring my sisters here and some left over."

"That's great news. Are you sure your sisters will come? They haven't written to you."

"I pray that they will. I pray with all my heart that they will find the courage to leave my uncle's house. I used to think that everyone's lives were like ours. That words of compassion were spoken at church but not practiced at home. Since coming here, I realize there are kind and generous people who live their faith as our Lord commanded and do more than pay it lip service. I'm so glad that I came."

"I'm glad that you came, too."

She blushed at his words, but nothing dimmed her happiness. "I have to get this in the mail to Mary. What will you do if three more women show up on your doorstep?"

"I'll hide."

She laughed as she rushed up the stairs. She didn't believe him. If only she knew the truth. The last thing on earth he wanted was a house full of women to look after. Just the thought of it made his blood run cold.

Chapter Twelve

Lizzie carried the coffeepot to the sink and began filling it with water. It had been two days since she put her quilt money in the mail to Mary. It should arrive today or tomorrow. How soon would she hear something?

Joe would be home before long. Would that mean less time working beside Carl? She enjoyed his company. She glanced out the window and noticed a speck of white in the green grass on the hillside beyond the barn. She leaned closer.

"A lamb. That's a lamb. Oh, my goodness, they're coming." She left the pot in the sink, ran out the door and raced down the hill to Carl's hut.

The door was open. He was seated on the edge of his bunk pulling on his boot.

"Carl, I saw one. I saw a lamb!"

A slow grin spread across his face. Why wasn't he as excited as she was? "We have been expecting them, Lizzie."

"You don't understand. It's out there all alone. The mother isn't with it. What if she has abandoned it?"

"Then you will get to bottle-feed one, but let's hope the mother is nearby."

Lizzie waited impatiently for him to pull on his other

boot. "I don't see how you can be so matter-of-fact when a baby has been left all alone out in the wilds."

Her patience gave out. She turned and ran back up the hill toward the pasture. She was out of breath and panting when she reached the baby sleeping quietly in the grass. She held her aching side as she sank to her knees beside it.

It was so small and so precious. She wanted to scoop it up and cuddle it in her arms, but she was afraid to touch it.

She heard a noise nearby and realized the mother was less than ten feet away on the other side of a bush. Her second lamb was busy nursing and twirling its tail.

"You didn't leave your baby. What a good mother you are."

Lizzie was still gazing at the beautiful sleeping creature when Carl joined her. He had a large navy blue bag slung over his shoulder. Duncan trotted at his heels.

Carl leaned down and picked up the lamb. It came awake with a start and struggled in his hands. Its frantic cries brought the ewe running back. She immediately began bleating loudly in protest. At a word from Carl, Duncan went out to distract her.

"What are you doing?" Lizzie demanded.

"When a lamb is born, some processing is required."

"What does that mean?"

"First, I checked to see if the lamb is healthy, and this one looks like she is. Then I put iodine on the navel to prevent infection. I give her a numbered ear tag because we will need to know which babies belong with which mothers. The numbers are easy enough to see when the lamb is standing still, but when they are running about, it's a lot harder, so I mark them with these waxy crayon sticks. I put the ewe's number on like so."

He demonstrated by marking the number forty-two on the lamb's left side with a yellow marking stick.

"If it's a single birth, the lamb will get marked with one stripe across its back from side to side. If it's a twin, two stripes and so on. Always mark them on the left side."

The mother continued to bellow her displeasure and lowered her head in a threatening gesture. Lizzie took a step away from Carl. "Are we done? She's very upset."

"Almost. I just have to put this rubber band over the tail. It's a bloodless way to dock the tail. The part below the rubber band will simply die and fall off in a couple of weeks. A shorter tail allows for cleaner sheep."

"I could've gone my entire life without knowing that fact."

He chuckled as he put the lamb on the ground. She quickly scurried to her mother's side. The mother stopped protesting and nuzzled her baby before moving away with it only to go through the entire process all over again when Carl caught and marked her other lamb.

He gave Duncan the command to gather, and the dog began herding the sheep and lambs toward the barn.

From that moment on, Lizzie had very little time to think about her sisters coming, about Joe getting out of the hospital and about how much she enjoyed working beside Carl. She was too busy with the newborn lambs.

Things went well until the weather took a turn for the worse. April began with an unusually cold and rainy week. It was a potentially disastrous combination for the newborns.

Some of the newly shorn mothers sought the shelter of the sheds and the barn, but some chose less suitable birthing places, such as dense thickets and groves of trees in the pasture.

Carl worked tirelessly to move the reluctant mothers and their newborns into the sheds. He built additional pens inside the barn and even moved the horses out so that he could turn their stalls into sheep maternity wards. Lizzie divided her time between bottle-feeding a pair of orphans every three hours and making sure Carl had food, hot coffee and warm, dry clothes.

When he wasn't assisting an ewe with a difficult birth or checking on the condition of the lambs, he combed the pastures for the few expectant mothers who had wandered away from the flock.

After three days of nonstop birthing, Lizzie could see how tired Carl was. "Please, let me help more. Tell me what to do."

"You're doing enough."

"I can do more."

"Lizzie, that's the trouble with you. You always think you can do more."

"Try me. If I can't manage, what have you lost?"

"Very well. In the smallest shed are the ewes that lambed three days ago. I need you to take hay to them and make sure they have plenty of water."

"I can do that. What else?"

"Add fresh straw to the pens if they look dirty. That will keep you busy for the next hour."

It didn't take her an hour to complete the tasks. She was back at his side as soon as she was able. He had delivered a set of twins from one ewe and was helping a second one deliver a lamb that was breech. "I've given them hay and water and new straw. Now what?"

"Check on number fifty-four. She had twins, but she wasn't letting one of them nurse a while ago. Let me know if they're both doing okay."

Lizzie walked down the aisle looking into the small pens where the mother sheep stood with their new babies until she saw the one whose ear tag was fifty-four. One of her babies was up and nursing. The other lay in a small huddle in the corner. Lizzie stepped into the pen and tried to rouse the little one, but it seemed too weak to stand. She rushed back to Carl.

"One of them is lying down and won't get up."

"Can you check his temperature for me?"

"If you tell me how." She felt so stupid. How could she be of help to him if she had to constantly run to him for information and instructions?

He grabbed a thermometer from his box of equipment and explained what she needed to do. "A lamb's temperature should be about 102°. If he's colder than that, take him to the warming boxes I have set up by the stove in the house." He extended the thermometer to her. She hesitated, then took it from him. This wasn't about Carl's shunning. This was about saving as many lambs as possible.

The lamb was much colder than he should have been. She bundled him up in a blanket and carried him up to the house. Carl had set four boxes around the stove in the kitchen. She put the lamb in one and made sure there was plenty of wood to last the night before going out to the barn again. She paused and groaned when she stepped outside. The bitter-cold rain was mixed with snow. How much worse could it get?

Carl's second ewe had successfully delivered her lambs. Both were trying to get to their feet while their mother nuzzled them. He gave Lizzie a tired smile. "These will be fine. I'm going back out to the hilltop pen. I saw two more ewes laboring up there an hour ago."

"Carl, it's snowing."

"Let's hope it doesn't last. Go back to the house. I'll be in shortly."

She did as he asked, but he wasn't back soon. She moved a lamp to the window to let him know she was still up in case he needed her, then she sat down in her grandfather's chair to wait. Carl would need some of the warm soup she had simmering on the stove when he came in.

Sometime later, she was jolted awake when the kitchen door flew open. Carl came in along with a flurry of wet snow. His black cowboy hat and coat were dusted with white. She hurried toward him. "You must be chilled to the bone."

He had something buttoned up inside his coat. Crossing to the stove, he knelt there. "I need your help. Bring me blankets, old ones if you have them, or towels."

He opened his jacket enough for her to see he had two tiny wet lambs bundled against his body for warmth.

Lizzie sprang into action. She raced up the stairs and pulled towels and blankets from the linen closet. Returning to Carl's side, she waited as he extracted one lamb and handed it to her. "Dry her good. She might make it. I'm not so sure about her brother."

"Did their mother reject them?" Lizzie knew it sometimes happened. She wrapped her baby in a towel and handed a second towel to Carl.

"Yes, she had triplets, but she would only nurse one."

Lizzie put the little one down for a minute and put several of the towels in the oven to warm. She went back and dried her charge as best she could. When the towels in the oven were warm, she wrapped the lambs in them.

"They'll need colostrum," Carl said. His baby remained lethargic.

Lizzie had learned it was the first milk the ewes produced and was essential to the newborn's health. A supply was kept frozen in a small propane-powered freezer in the barn. "I'll get some and warm it up."

She handed him her lamb and jumped to her feet. Carl caught her hand as she walked by and looked up at her.

"Thank you. For everything you've done. I don't know what I would have done without you."

"I'm glad I was here to help."

"So am I."

He slowly released her hand and she missed the comfort of his touch more than she imagined was possible. "You're an amazing man, Carl. I don't know how you do it. I admire your dedication, your skill, your selflessness. This has been a time I will never forget."

After that, the following days became something of a blur for Lizzie. Two more orphans joined the collection in the kitchen. Each morning at five o'clock, Lizzie rose, made a mug of strong tea and checked on the orphaned lambs. Most times, Carl was already there feeding them their breakfast before getting his own. It was amusing to see him seated on the floor with a baby bottle in each hand and lambs climbing on his lap in the hopes of being next.

After the babies were fed, she and Carl walked together to the pasture looking for lambs that had arrived during the past few hours or for ewes that were in obvious distress. When they found lambs, they would carry them back to the barn with their anxious mothers following alongside.

During the peak lambing season, the new arrivals came fast and furious. The ewes delivered late at night, in the early hours and throughout the day. At times, it seemed to Lizzie that there were baby sheep in every nook and cranny on the farm.

Through the rough parts, it seemed to her as if Carl never slept. She knew, because she slept very little herself. But no matter how tired or busy she was, she always made time to run down to the end of the lane and collect the mail. Every afternoon she hoped for a message from her friend or her sisters, but none came. Slowly, her hope began to fade.

The bad weather finally broke on Sunday morning and the sun came out. Lizzie had never been so glad to lift her face to the warming rays and simply soak them up. It was the off Sunday, so there was no need to travel to church.

Carl opened the gates of one shed and let the ewes with lambs several days old out into a larger enclosure. The ewes, thrilled to be back outside, got busy eating the new green grass where the sun had melted patches free of snow. The lambs, not used to being ignored, discovered each other.

They gathered in a bunch and began butting each other. Suddenly, they broke and ran, jumping and leaping for the sheer joy of it over the ground until they noticed that they had strayed too far from their mothers. In what looked like a race, they all came galloping back. Only an occasional mother even raised her head from the green grass to check on them.

Lizzie leaned on the fence beside Carl and watched it all with a feeling of deep contentment. "'This is the day which the Lord hath made; we will rejoice and be glad in it.'"

"Psalm 118:24," he said quietly.

Her heart turned over as she looked at him. "Isn't it wonderful how God brings us joy in the simplest ways? It's a sign of His endless love."

She didn't turn away from the warm look that filled his eyes. "You almost make me believe that, Lizzie."

Drawn to the change she sensed in him, she stepped closer and laid her hand over his heart. "Then I'm happy to be His instrument. The Lamb of God gave up His life on the cross so that we might know salvation. It is up to each of us to cherish or to deny that gift."

He looked away. "It's more complicated than that."

She let her hand fall to her side. "When you come right down to it, it's not."

Bracing his forearms on the fence, he stared at the ground. "There are other people involved."

"God didn't create us to live alone. There are always people who touch our lives, for better or for worse. None of them can change God's love for you or for me. It is eternal."

"So they say, but it doesn't feel like it to me. I'd better finish checking the pens in the barn. We have a dozen mothers-in-waiting left."

He walked away, leaving her aching for his pain. He was so lost. If only there was some way to help him.

When the last pregnant ewe gave birth, Lizzie gave a huge sigh of relief. After more than a week of nonstop work, the worst was finally behind them.

On Friday, just like clockwork, another letter arrived for Carl, but this time there was a letter from Mary, as well. Lizzie had been on the verge of giving up hope. Clara's wedding was less than a week away.

She quickly opened her letter and read the bitter news. Mary had been unable to see her sisters, but she would keep trying to get Lizzie's money to them.

Lizzie nearly screamed with frustration. She wanted to hear from her family so badly, while Carl ignored letters from his. It wasn't fair.

Back in the kitchen, Lizzie started supper, but she was drawn to Carl's letter. She picked it up and spent a long time looking at the envelope. Was Carl ignoring an olive branch extended by his family? Lizzie had no way of knowing unless she opened the letter and read it.

It was so tempting. Carl would never know if she burned it for him. She laid the letter on the kitchen table with the rest of the mail and went to the stove. Turning back quickly, she snatched the envelope up and held it in the steam rising from the eggs she was boiling to make egg-salad sandwiches. The steam burned her fingers before the glue on the envelope gave way.

Ashamed of herself, she put the letter back where it belonged and continued fixing supper. A dozen times, she glanced at the table as she worked. Finally, she covered the distraction with a kitchen towel.

It was not her letter. It was not her life. To read or to destroy the correspondence was up to Carl. She removed the towel and put the letter under the newspaper.

It was nearly dark by the time he came in. She was seated at the table with a cup of coffee in her hands. "Do we have any sick ones?"

He hung his cowboy hat on a wooden peg beside the door. "Not yet. At least, none that I've found, but I think we're missing one."

"An ewe or a lamb?"

"A lamb. Number eighty-three had twins, but she's only got one lamb with her now."

"Maybe one of the others stole it." An ewe without a lamb of her own would sometimes try to steal another's baby.

"Maybe. Is there any coffee left?"

"In the pot. It's fresh."

He poured a cup, blew on it to cool it and took a sip. "Before you leave, will you please teach Joe how to make good coffee? I can't go back to drinking the shoe polish that he makes."

She chuckled. "I will do my best."

He looked around the house. "This is nice."

She looked around to see what he was referring to but didn't see anything unusual. "What's nice?"

"Coming into a clean house with supper simmering

on the stove. You have no idea what a difference it makes after a long, hard day of work outside."

"I'm happy that I can ease your way, for you work very hard. Supper will be ready in about twenty minutes." She pointed to the pile of mail on the corner of the table. "The paper came today, if you want to read it while you wait."

"After supper."

Lizzie bit her bottom lip to keep from mentioning his letter. Maybe this time he would open it. She got up and began to set the table.

When they finished the meal, Carl took the mail into the other room while Lizzie cleaned up. She was putting away the last plate when he walked past her, opened the firebox of the stove and dropped the letter in.

"Supper was good. Thank you. I'll see you in the morning." He walked to the pegs by the door and put on his coat and hat.

Her heart sank. Someone was desperately reaching out to him, and he was just as desperately keeping that someone at bay. She couldn't remain silent any longer. "If you mark them Return to Sender, perhaps she will stop writing."

He paused with his hand on the doorknob, but didn't look at her. "I tried that once, but it didn't work."

Lizzie heard the pain in his voice and wanted to throw her arms around him and hold him close. It was impossible for her to do so, but knowing that didn't lessen her desire to comfort him. "I think only someone who loves you very much would remain so persistent."

He walked out and closed the door behind him without a word.

Carl continued toward his hut in the dark. He knew the path by heart. He didn't need to see where he was going.

Duncan walked beside him. He looked down at the dog, who had been his best friend for a long time. "Lizzie is like a dog with a bone about those letters. In fact, she's worse than you are. She's not going to bury it and leave it alone."

She was every bit as persistent as Jenna was. He wished now that he'd never told his sister where he was staying.

He sat down on the chair outside his door and stared out over the pastures. The white sheep dotting the hillsides stood out in stark contrast to the dark ground. They looked like little stars that had fallen from the sky. Duncan lay down beside Carl and licked his paw.

Only a month ago, Carl would have enjoyed the peaceful calm of a night like this, but tonight he didn't appreciate the pastoral serenity. Tonight, he was restless and edgy.

Lizzie was eager to find out more about him. He saw it every time she looked at him. He heard it in her voice each time she mentioned his letters. She cared for him. He saw that in her eyes, too, even as he struggled to keep his feelings for her hidden.

If he gave in and told her the truth, what would he see in her eyes then? How would she look at him when she learned he had killed a man? Would he see horror? Revulsion? Pity?

He leaned his head back against the wall. Maybe it was time for him to move on. It would be best to go before he fell deeper in love with the amazing little woman with smiling eyes. A woman he could never hold.

Duncan suddenly sprang to his feet and growled deep in his throat. The hair on his neck stood up as every muscle in his body tensed.

Carl stared out into the darkness, trying to see what had riled his dog. It took a bit, but finally he saw a darker shadow streaking along the hillside on the opposite side of the creek. He stood up to get a better look. Was it a coyote or a dog?

He realized as the animal crested the hill that it carried one of his lambs in its mouth. A second later, it was lost from sight. Duncan took off after it at a run.

Chapter Thirteen

The day Joe came home from the hospital was the day of Clara's wedding.

Carl watched Lizzie try to keep a brave face as they waited for the van that would bring Joe home, but he could see the strain she was under. The days since she had mailed her quilt money had gone by without a single word from her sisters. He had no idea what had gone wrong with her plan, but she wore the look of a woman who was barely hanging on to hope.

He wondered how long it would be before he saw her smile again.

Outside, the sun was shining. A soft breeze turned the windmill beside the barn and stirred the new grass in the pastures in small, undulating waves. Carl had moved the entire flock close to the house, but he was still losing a lamb every other night.

Lizzie became as nervous as a June bug in a henhouse when the van finally rolled in. And well she should be. She was the reason Joe ended up in the hospital in the first place. Carl knew Joe had forgiven her, but he was worried that Joe might not let her forget it anytime soon.

When the driver got out and opened the door, she rushed

down the steps with an offer of help. To Carl's surprise, Joe calmly accepted Lizzie's offer and allowed her to help him out of the car. He walked haltingly with a walker, but managed well enough.

With Carl on one side and Lizzie on the other, they were able to help Joe up the steps and into the house. Once inside, he looked around and sighed deeply. "You have no idea how good it feels to come home."

"I have your room ready, Daadi. Would you like to lie down now?"

"No, I'm sick of being in bed. I would like to sit in my chair for a while."

"Of course." She hovered beside him as he crossed into the living room and sank with a deep sigh of relief into his overstuffed chair. She quickly arranged a footstool and pillows so he could elevate his legs. She had been paying close attention to the home-care instructions the hospital had mailed to her.

Carl was delighted to see his friend looking so well, if a bit weak and worn-out. "You have two hundred and seventy-eight new lambs."

"How many ewes did we lose?"

"Only two."

"And how many lambs have we lost? Every day I watched the rain running down the windows of the hospital I was thinking about my poor babies out in such weather."

"We didn't lose any to the weather."

"Are you serious?"

"Lizzie has been busy bottle-feeding six of them."

"That's a lot of work," Joe said, looking at her with admiration.

"I don't mind. They're adorable, but any praise must go to Carl." She turned her earnest eyes in his direction and he saw admiration in them, but also something more. He saw an echo of the way he felt about her.

"Carl worked day and night to make sure the sheep had the best possible care. He went out in a snowstorm to look for lambs. He brought back two that lived because of his dedication."

Carl decided the bad news could wait until after Joe had rested.

Joe looked around the room. "Where's Duncan? I didn't see him when we came in. He normally raises a ruckus when there's a car around."

"I have him on guard duty with the flock."

Lizzie knelt beside Joe. "We can talk about this later. Daadi, you need to rest."

"Coyotes?" Joe's sharp eyes drilled into Carl and ignored Lizzie.

"A big one."

"How many has he gotten?"

"Four."

Joe pushed himself up straighter in the chair. "You know what has to be done?"

"I won't touch a gun, Joe. You know that."

"A gun?" Lizzie's eyes widened with shock. "You aren't thinking about shooting it, are you?"

Joe gave her an exasperated look. "A coyote that starts killing sheep won't stop. It has to be put down."

"Isn't there another way?"

"What other way?" Joe asked.

"I don't know, but it doesn't deserve to be shot without trying something else. We could trap it."

Carl remained silent. Each word of Lizzie's protest cut like a knife. She couldn't bear the thought of him killing a wild predator. How appalled would she be if she knew the truth about his deed? He grew sick at the thought.

Joe patted her hand. "Women! Soft hearts and soft heads. My rifle is in my room, Carl. You know I wouldn't ask you to do this if I could do it myself. The sheep can't defend themselves."

Carl nodded. Lizzie's eyes begged him not to do it. He looked away. He didn't want to kill anything, but better that she hate him for thinking about shooting a coyote than to know the truth. Maybe this way she would see that he wasn't worth trying to save.

Maybe he could stop loving her if she stopped looking at him as if he was her hero.

Lizzie couldn't decipher the expression on Carl's face. It was as if he had suddenly turned to stone. There was a lack of life in his eyes that troubled her.

"I'm surprised your sisters aren't here," Joe said, pulling Lizzie's attention away from Carl.

"I have not heard from them," she said. Her disappointment and worry were too heavy to hide.

"Oh. I thought they had the means to join you. Naomi Wadler stopped in to see me and she mentioned that you were selling a quilt to pay for their bus fare. Did you change your mind?"

"I sent them money. However, it may have been too late or my uncle may have intercepted it. Clara's wedding was moved up after I left. The ceremony was to take place today."

He sank back in his chair. Lines of fatigue and pain appeared on his face. "So she is married to him, the man you don't like and don't trust. I'm sorry for her. And for you."

"It must be God's will for her. Perhaps her kindness will change his heart and make him a husband she can respect and admire."

Joe laid a hand on Lizzie's head. "I have been a fool

and so I must pay the price, but I'm sorry you must pay it, too. What will you do now?"

"I love it here. The people of this community are so warm and loving. I even like the sheep now much more than I did when we had to shear them."

"But you aren't going to stay," Carl said softly.

"I can't leave them there. I have to go back." She tried to gauge his reaction to her decision, but she couldn't. Tears blurred her vision.

"You can't go until I'm fit," Joe grumbled.

She rose to her feet. "Of course not. I promised I would stay as long as you need me. I should go feed the orphans. Carl will stay with you to make sure you don't overdo it."

"I don't need a babysitter."

Lizzie escaped out the door before she heard Carl's reply. He was used to handling Joe. She knew he would manage without her. She gathered the baby bottles and milk replacer and went down to the barn where the orphans lived now. After only a week, they had outgrown their warming boxes. They slept now in an empty stall at the back of the barn.

She sat down on the hay among them, and as they pushed and shoved for her attention, she held their soft bodies close one at a time and gave in to her tears.

She was responsible for her own heartbreak. She knew better than to fall for Carl, but that hadn't stopped her from embracing every dear quality he possessed. It was so easy to love him.

In the long years ahead, she would look back on their days together and remember what it was like to share the joys and pains of everyday life with him. She would never forget the way he made her feel.

If only she knew he would find his way back to his faith, she wouldn't mind leaving so much.

After she finished feeding the orphans, she returned to the house and went up to her room. She pulled a sheet of paper from the small desk by the window and sat down to write a letter. She raised her pen to her mouth and nibbled on the end of it as she considered what to say. Finally, she started writing.

Dear Jenna,
You don't know me, but I am a friend of Carl King's. He lives and works on my grandfather's sheep farm here in Ohio. I have only recently moved here, but I soon became aware that you write to Carl every week. I hesitate to tell you this, but Carl burns your letters without reading them. He does not know that I am writing to you.

When I first met Carl, he told me he is in the Bann, but he will not say why he has been shunned. His situation weighs heavily on my heart for I have come to care for him a great deal.

Lizzie lifted her pen from the paper. She didn't just care for Carl. She loved him. She always would.

A tear splashed onto the page as she began writing again.

Carl keeps all rules of our faith, except that he will not attend our services. I have seen him standing outside of our place of worship, close enough to hear the preaching and singing and yet not be a part of it. His separation from God is painful to see, for I know that it is painful to him, too.

It is my hope that with some understanding of Carl's past, I can help him to return to the faith he clearly loves. He refuses to tell me anything. I'm hoping that you will. I value Carl's friendship and his trust. I risk losing that which is most dear to me by writing to you, but what Carl stands to gain is so much more important.

Please forgive me if you find this intrusion into your affairs offensive. I mean no harm. I don't do this lightly, but only with the very best of intentions. If you do not answer this letter, I will not bother you again.
Your sister in Christ,
Elizabeth Barkman

When she finished the brief missive, she folded it and slipped it into an envelope before she could change her mind. Carl was stuck in limbo. He couldn't move forward with his life until he had received forgiveness from someone in his past. If that person was the author of his letters, then perhaps letting her know how much Carl desperately needed her forgiveness would spark their reconciliation.

She didn't delude herself into thinking Carl would approve of her actions. He would be furious with her.

She composed a second letter. This one was to her sisters telling them that she would be returning in a few weeks. As much as she longed to see them, she dreaded returning to life in her uncle's home. How would she bear it after knowing a better way existed?

She took her letters down to the mailbox in the early afternoon when she knew the mailman was due to go by. If there was a letter from Mary or from her sisters and they were coming, Lizzie wouldn't send the ones she had written, for it meant she would be staying in Hope Springs.

The postman handed over the mail. "I see you have a new crop of lambs out there. How did it go?"

"Busy. Joe is home from the hospital now. You are welcome to bring your son and pick a lamb whenever you like."

"We're going to be gone on a family vacation for a week, but we'll do it sometime after we get back. Do you want to mail those letters?" He pointed to the ones in her hand.

She finished looking through a handful of junk mail. There was nothing from her family. She nodded. "I guess I do."

Her conscience pricked her all through the day and kept her awake until long into the night. She had no right to interfere in Carl's personal affairs. It was prideful on her part to think what she said would matter.

Where was Clara tonight? Was she at the home of her new husband? How was he treating her?

Lizzie pulled her pillow over her face to shut out her fears. It didn't work.

Carl attributed Lizzie's long face to her grief at not being able to help her family. She didn't say a word as they finished the morning chores and turned out the youngest lambs with their mothers. She barely spoke to the orphans as they clamored for her attention.

On the way back to the house, he said, "You're awfully quiet today."

"Am I?

"Do you have something on your mind?"

"A lot of things."

"Such as?"

"Number ninety-four doesn't seem to have enough milk for her triplets. We may need to supplement one of them with milk replacer."

"Just what we need, another mouth to feed in the orphan pen."

"I'll take care of moving him this afternoon," Lizzie said as she walked up the steps ahead of him. She opened the front door and stopped so abruptly that he almost ran into her. She shrieked, dropped the bucket she was carrying and charged into the room. Carl rushed in behind her to see what was wrong.

Suddenly, the room echoed with shrieks as three women rushed to embrace Lizzie. They were all laughing, crying and hugging each other. Joe stood leaning on his walker on the far side of the room.

Carl skirted the women and moved to stand beside him. "I take it these are the rest of your granddaughters?"

"They are. Have you ever heard such a noisy bunch? They're worse than a barn full of sheep."

Although Joe tried to hide it with his gruff words, Carl heard the happiness in his voice. Carl was happy, too, that Lizzie's dream had come true. Now she wouldn't be leaving.

Lizzie had tears of joy rolling down her face but she didn't care. "How did you get here? I thought the wedding was yesterday. I didn't know when I would ever see you again."

Greta said, "The wedding *was* yesterday, but the bride failed to show up for it."

Clara grasped Lizzie's hands. "I don't know how I can ever thank you. We would have come sooner, but we didn't know Mary had the money you sent until the morning of the wedding. Uncle Morris wouldn't let us have visitors until then."

Betsy wrapped her arm around Clara's waist. "Mary showed up at the house demanding that she be allowed to attend Clara on her wedding day. There were already people at the house, so I think uncle didn't want to look bad in front of them by saying no."

Greta took up the tale. "The moment Mary was in the room with us, she gave us your letters and then handed each of us a bus ticket and said that her buggy was waiting for us outside."

"We climbed out the window and drove into town as fast as we could. We barely made it to the bus station on time," Betsy added with a dramatic flourish.

Lizzie pressed a hand to her heart. "Oh, I wish I had been there to see it."

Clara shook her head. "If you had been there, none of us would be here now. You showed us the way. Your courage gave us courage."

"I prayed that you had guessed what I was trying to do and that you didn't think I had simply run away."

The three sisters exchanged glances. Greta laid a hand on Lizzie's shoulder. "We knew."

Joe came forward with his walker. "Now that all the screaming is over, I hope a man can have his lunch in peace."

Lizzie drew a deep breath. "*Ja,* Daadi. We will have your lunch ready in no time."

She caught sight of Carl as he was slipping out the back door. She left her sisters and caught up with him on the back porch. "Where are you going? You must stay and meet my family."

"Another time." His voice held a sad quality that made her want to fold her arms around him.

"But I want them to meet you. Stay for lunch with us."

"Half the table won't be big enough for all of you, Lizzie." It was a pointed reminder that he could not eat with them.

"They don't have to know. I won't say anything. They will think you are an Englisch hired hand."

"But I will know, and you will know, Lizzie. I'm glad your plan worked. I'm really happy for you."

"Will you be in for supper?"

"I don't think so."

It was then that Lizzie realized the arrival of her sisters spelled the end of her time alone with Carl. "You have to eat."

"We've had this conversation before. You like to feed people."

"It's what I'm good at."

"Fix me a sandwich, then. I'm going to camp out in the pasture and try to keep that coyote from killing any more lambs.

"Will you shoot it?"

"Not if I don't have to."

"*Goot.* That makes me feel better."

"It's a wild animal, Lizzie."

"Every life is valuable, Carl. We are all God's creatures."

She saw him flinch at her words. Maybe she was being too hard on him. The lambs were God's creatures, too. She didn't want any of them to die. "You'll do the right thing. I know that."

He nodded and walked away, but she had the feeling that she had somehow let him down.

Lizzie spent the rest of the day surrounded by her sisters. They were eager to hear about everything that she had done since leaving home. Her stories about shearing alpacas and sheep had them all laughing. Her grandfather sat on the edge of their group and added a few stories of his own. When she recounted Naomi's stories about their mother, she caught a glint of tears in Joe's eyes.

She made up sandwiches for Carl, but he never came to the house to pick them up, so she left them in the refrigerator for him and left a note telling him where they were on the kitchen table.

The next morning, he came in while her sisters and Joe were all seated around the kitchen table. Carl's face was grave. He held a bloody bundle in his arms. Lizzie jumped to her feet. "Are you hurt?"

"No, but this poor little girl is." He unwrapped part of the cloth to show them a lamb with a gaping wound on its hind leg.

Lizzie immediately came over to examine the animal. "It's a deep laceration. She's going to need stitches. We should get her to a vet right away. She may go into shock from blood loss. We need to keep her warm." She lifted the lamb out of Carl's arms and moved to stand close to the stove with it.

Greta filled a hot-water bottle and gave it to Lizzie, who tucked it in with the lamb. She looked at Carl. "Was it the coyote?"

"Yes. It came within fifty feet of me. It has no fear of humans. I think it's a coydog. A coyote and dog cross. That's why it's so big. It's not killing for food. It's killing the sheep for fun. Duncan drove it off but not before it had a chance to kill one and maim this poor little one. I'll go hitch up the wagon."

Joe said, "Take the buggy. My trotter is faster than the pony. Greta, you and Lizzie take the lamb to the vet. Carl, you and I need to figure out what we're going to do about this."

"We should notify the sheriff. The animal is big enough to start attacking cattle, too, if it hasn't already."

"All right. Go call him. Then take my gun out and practice with it. I'm not going to lose my whole lamb crop. I can't afford to lose even one more."

Carl knew Joe was right, but the last thing he wanted in his hands was another gun.

Chapter Fourteen

❧

Sheriff Bradley came to the farm, and Carl filed a report with him. The sheriff suggested Carl put a notice in several of the local newspapers with a description of the coydog in the unlikely event that it was a pet and not a wild animal. After an entire week passed without another attack, Carl joined Lizzie and Joe in the living room.

Carl leaned forward and propped his forearms on his thighs. "Maybe the sheriff was right and the coydog isn't wild. Maybe the owner read about his pet in the paper and decided it was time to keep Fido in his kennel at night."

Joe nodded. "Another explanation is that someone else took care of the problem for us."

"I'd rather think that he's home and safe with his family," Lizzie said.

Carl looked around. "Speaking of family, where are the girls?"

"Clara has gone to meet Adrian and Faith and see if she wants the job they have to offer. Sally Yoder took Betsy to meet the Sutter family."

He frowned at her. "Wasn't that the job you were going to take?"

"I would have been happy to work for them, but I think Betsy will be happier."

"You just want to stay here and boss me around," Joe grumbled.

"You're right. That's exactly why I want to stay. It's time for you to do some more walking. You can't sit around all day like a king on his throne."

Joe muttered under his breath, but he stood up with his walker. "I'll be outside with Greta. I've never seen anyone so happy to be hoeing in the dirt. My garden will be twice its size when she's done. Lizzie, I meant to tell you what a good job you've done with that crippled lamb. She's almost as good as new."

"Danki." Lizzie was smiling as she watched Joe make his way out the door.

"Is this what you imagined it would be like when they came?" Carl asked.

By mutual consent, they had avoided spending time alone in each other's company. She kept her eyes lowered modestly. She rarely looked him in the eyes anymore. "This is so much more wonderful than I dreamed. It fills my heart with joy to see them meeting new people and going to new places."

"It does my heart good to see you happy, Lizzie."

She turned her face aside. "You should not say such things."

"I know it's not proper, but I wanted you to hear it anyway. You didn't used to be so proper."

"Things were different then. Now I have my sisters to think of."

He'd done a lot of soul-searching while he was patrolling Joe's pastures over the past few nights. Soul-searching and longing for a life within the community that had welcomed Lizzie and her sisters with such joy and kindness.

He had arrived at an answer. He hoped. He would go home and beg forgiveness for Sophia's death and the killing of the soldier from his parents, his siblings and his church. If they granted him what he sought, then the past would stay in the past. When a sinner was forgiven, the sin need never be mentioned again. Lizzie would never have to know what he had done.

"I'm going away for a while, Lizzie."

She looked up and locked eyes with him. "For how long?"

"I'm not sure."

"But you'll be back."

"It is my dearest hope to return to you as soon as possible." He couldn't say too much, but he longed to tell her of his love.

"Are you going home, Carl?"

"Ja."

She smiled. *"Goot.* I miss you already. When are you leaving?"

"The day after tomorrow."

She reached out and laid her hand on his. "Then I wish you Godspeed."

He left the house feeling hope for the first time in five long years. Lizzie had brought hope into his life. She was the sign he had been waiting for.

"Is that a car I hear?" Joe asked from his chair. The crippled lamb, now known as Patience, was asleep on his lap. Greta was out checking the pasture with Carl and Duncan. She expected them back at any time.

Lizzie looked out the living-room window. "It is a car. Maybe it's one of your therapists."

"I don't have physical therapy scheduled for today."

She pointed a finger at him. "That doesn't mean you get to skip your exercises."

"Nag, nag. Don't worry, I'll do them. I don't intend to be glued to a walker for the rest my life. Don't just stand there. Go see who it is."

Lizzie brushed off the front of her apron, straightened her *kapp* and went to the door. An Amish woman and an ebony-skinned girl of about thirteen dressed in Englisch clothes emerged from the backseat.

The girl darted away from the car and came running up the steps. "Is Kondoo Mtu here? Where is he? I want to thank him for the good life he has given me."

Her thick accent kept Lizzie from understanding who she was looking for. "You must have the wrong house. There's no one by that name here."

The Amish woman came and stood behind the girl with her hands on her shoulders. "*Kondoo Mtu* means 'Sheep Man.' When Carl would say, *'Ja. Ja,'* to her, it sounded like 'Baa. Baa.' Hence, Sheep Man. Hello, I'm Jenna King. And this bundle of energy is my adopted daughter, Christina. Her English is improving, but she still has trouble with many of our words. Are you Elizabeth Barkman?"

"I am." Lizzie wasn't sure what else to say. She had expected a letter in response to the one she wrote, not a face-to-face visit.

"Who is it?" Joe shouted from the living room.

"I'm Carl's sister," the woman said with a knowing smile.

Lizzie went weak in the knees with relief. Not a wife. A sister. "Oh, I'm very glad to meet you. Come in and meet my grandfather."

"Where is Carl?"

"He's out checking the lambs. He should be in soon. He still doesn't know I wrote to you."

"I'm very glad you did. When you wrote that Carl had burned my letters, I was hurt. I knew I had to come see him in person. Besides, I wanted to meet the woman who cares so much about him. "

Lizzie's face grew hot. "I do care about him. He's a good man."

"Then perhaps together we can help him find his way back to his family and his faith. You said Carl hasn't told you why he was shunned. Is that still true?"

"He won't speak of it."

"It's a tragic story, but one I think he must share with you himself. If he isn't ready to do that, then my coming here may have been a mistake."

Was it a mistake? Lizzie prayed she hadn't done the wrong thing by writing to Jenna. "I don't think it was a mistake for you to come here. Carl told me yesterday that he planned to go home."

Relief brightened Jenna's eyes. "That's good to hear."

"Please come inside while you wait for him."

"Danki." Jenna held out her hand and Christina dashed to her side. Together, they entered the house.

Lizzie scanned the hillside, looking for Carl. There wasn't any sign of him. A sick feeling settled in her stomach. What was he going to say when he found out what she'd done?

In the living room, Jenna and Christina took a seat on the sofa. Lizzie introduced them to her grandfather. Christina couldn't sit still. She was up and down a dozen times to pet the lamb in Joe's lap and look out the window. Jenna gave Joe an apologetic smile. "I'm sorry. She's just so excited to see Carl again. She hasn't seen him since they came back from Africa."

"Carl was in Africa?" Joe was clearly shocked.

Lizzie leaned forward knowing she was finally going to learn about Carl's past.

Jenna nodded. "We had a younger sister named Sophia. She was drawn to missionary work. She chose not to be baptized and left home to work with a Mennonite group in Africa. She fell in love with a young man working there and they decided to marry. Sophia wanted someone from the family to attend her wedding. You can't blame her. My mother's health wasn't good. I didn't want to go, so Carl went."

Christina beamed. "He came to my village. He made us all laugh. He made Sophie happy. We liked him."

Jenna's eyes grew sad. "The wedding never took place. The village was raided by rebel soldiers and everyone was killed, including Christina's parents. Carl and Christina were the only survivors."

Christina left the window to stand in front of Lizzie. "The bad men came and shoot, shoot, shoot. Kondoo Mtu, he saved me."

Jenna leaned forward. "Christina, no! We don't speak of this."

But the excited child continued, "He get gun and kill the bad man who killed my father. He shoot him dead. We hide. Then more soldiers find Sophia and my mother. They kill them, too."

Lizzie went rigid with shock. A loud buzzing filled her ears. No Amish man would raise a gun to another human. She couldn't believe what she was hearing.

Jenna jumped to her feet and put her arms around Christina. Regret was etched deeply in her face. "I'm so sorry, Lizzie. This isn't how I wanted you to find out."

Lizzie couldn't draw a breath. It was as if the air was gone from the room. "Carl killed a man? He shot him?"

"Yes, I did," Carl said from the doorway.

Lizzie turned to stare at him, but she couldn't speak. Never had she imagined such horrible things could happen to someone she knew.

Christina dashed across the room. She threw her arms around him. "Kondoo Mtu, do you remember me?"

"Yes, I remember you." He kissed her cheek and she beamed at him.

"Thank you for bringing me to Jenna. She is good lady."

"I know. Why don't you go down to the barn and tell the lady there that you would like to feed the lambs? Tell her that I sent you. Her name is Greta."

When the child did as he asked, he looked straight at Lizzie. "Now you know."

What should she say? She hadn't been prepared for anything like this.

After a long minute, he looked down and gave a deep sigh. Then he turned and started to walk away.

Behind her, Lizzie heard Jenna call his name. He stopped. He spoke without turning around. "You shouldn't have come here, Jenna. Why did you?"

"She's here because I wrote to her," Lizzie admitted. Why wouldn't he look at them?

"You shouldn't have done that, Lizzie." He shook his head sadly. "I knew this was too good to last."

He walked away without another word, leaving Lizzie in shock and wondering what to do next.

Jenna put her arm around Lizzie's shoulders. "I'm so very sorry."

Lizzie managed to speak without breaking down in tears. "Don't be. It's Carl's choice to remain apart." Apart from her and the love she would so willingly give him.

"Come, sit down and I'll tell you the rest of the story."

Lizzie followed her back to the sofa.

When they were seated, Jenna said, "Carl returned to

our family a broken man. He was haunted by his actions and Sophia's death. At night, he would wake up screaming. We did all we could to console him, but it didn't help. He refused to ask for forgiveness. He didn't believe he deserved it. He stopped going to church services and eventually our bishop had no choice but to place him in the Bann until he repented. Instead, Carl left without telling anyone where he was going."

Joe sighed heavily and straightened his leg with a grimace of pain. "He didn't have a destination in mind. He told me he'd been walking the back roads and getting odd jobs to get by. It wasn't until he found a starving puppy that he decided to stay in one place. The Lord blessed me when He led Carl here."

Jenna smiled at him. "Our family is grateful for your generosity. Carl didn't contact us until two years ago. He called the business where I work. I thought it signaled a change for the better, something we had all been praying for. I wrote him every week thinking that reading my letters would help him see that we still loved him and wanted him to come home."

"He would have gone home if I hadn't interfered." Lizzie bit her lower lip, rose from the sofa and went outside.

After hearing Jenna relate the entire sad story, she finally understood a little of what Carl had gone through. She gathered her shattered emotions and went to find him and beg his forgiveness.

Following the path that led to his place, she tried to imagine what she would say to him. Nothing formed in her mind. It was as if a dark curtain had been pulled across her emotions. She paused in the open door of the shepherd's hut. He had his back to her. He was stuffing his clothes in a black duffel bag.

"Carl, I must speak to you."

He stopped what he was doing and straightened, but he didn't turn around. "Don't bother. I already know what you have to say."

She took a step inside the door. "I don't think you do."

"You know what I did. You don't have to say anything. I'm leaving. All I ask is that you take good care of Duncan for me."

"All I ask is that you turn around and look at me."

His shoulders slumped. "Don't make this harder, Lizzie."

If he wouldn't turn around, she would just have to apologize to his back. "It is not my intention to make anything harder, but my good intentions have not turned out as I hoped. I'm sorry for interfering, Carl. I shouldn't have written to Jenna without your knowledge. I betrayed your trust, and I'm truly sorry. I wanted you to confide in me."

"When is the right time to tell the woman you love that you're a murderer?" He closed his eyes and bowed his head.

In two quick strides, she crossed the room and cupped his face with her hands. There were tears on his cheeks. "I cannot begin to comprehend the horror and the terror you faced. Under such ghastly circumstances, a man does not know how he will react until he is in the situation."

"Our faith tells us what a man must do, no matter what circumstances he faces. 'Thou shalt not kill.'"

He pulled free of her touch and resumed packing. "I made a choice. I decided another man's life was less valuable than mine, or Christina's. I became his judge and jury, and I snuffed out his life in the blink of an eye. In his fellow soldier's fury to avenge him, I brought a terrible fate upon my sister and the women with her. They all died because of me. I'm the one who should have died, not Sophia and her friends. I see them in my dreams. I can't get their faces out of my head. I never wanted you to know what I did."

"Don't torture yourself. I know your sister has forgiven you."

"Go back to the house, Lizzie. I don't want to see you again. I can't bear the way you look at me now. Tell Jenna to go home. I don't want to see her, either."

"But you told me yesterday that you intended to go home."

"I was wrong to think I could. I see now there is no reason to go back. Nothing has changed for me."

Lizzie struggled to find the right thing to say, but she was at a loss. She didn't know how to help him deal with his crushing burden of guilt. "I was shocked by what I heard. I'll admit that."

"Can you say your feelings for me haven't changed?"

"Give me some time to come to grips with this."

"That's what I thought."

"Please, do not judge me harshly. I'm not sure how I feel, but I do care about you. I forgive you for what you did. There's no question about that in my heart. Have you forgiven yourself?"

"I don't know how to do that."

She couldn't get through to him. "Where will you go?"

He stopped packing and raised his face to the ceiling. "Away." Then he began stuffing his clothes into his pack again.

"Carl, don't shut me out."

"Go away, Lizzie. Please."

Lizzie felt as if the ground had vanished from beneath her. She couldn't reach through the prison walls he had erected around his heart. With no other choice, she left and went back to the house. When she reached the porch steps, she broke down and sobbed as if her heart were breaking.

Because it was.

Carl stood in the hut after Lizzie left without moving. It hurt to breathe. He had no place to go. He was adrift without a compass of any kind. What now? Where could he find a hole deep enough to hide in so that he never had to face himself again? Where would he find peace?

Nowhere. So why was he running away? What was he running to?

He raked a hand through his hair. It wasn't right to leave while Joe was crippled. He owed the man too much.

If he left, he would never see Lizzie again. She didn't hate him, but had he lost her love?

He fell to his knees with his hands at his sides and gave vent to his pain. "God, why are You doing this to me? Because I dared to love her? You made her the way she is. How could I not love her?"

He had no idea how long he knelt slumped on the stone floor. His legs grew numb. His eyes burned from the tears that streamed down his face. All he could say was "God, help me. I'm sorry. I'm sorry. Forgive me."

Gradually, his despair faded and a gentle calm replaced it. He felt something rough on his face. He realized that Duncan was licking his tears.

He wrapped his arms around the dog and held on. "Am I forgiven? Have you been the sign from Him all along but I refused to see it? Was Joe the sign I had God's forgiveness? Is it Lizzie? How many signs do I need to tell me that life is good if I choose to live it as He wills?"

As He wills, not as Carl King would have it.

For the first time, he understood that he couldn't hide from what he had done. He had to accept his failure, not wallow in it, and go forward. He would face other tests in his life. Some great and some small, but all were by the will of God. He prayed for the strength to meet them with humility and peace in his heart.

Struggling to his feet, he walked to the door, surprised to see it was almost dark. Duncan growled low in his throat. The sounds of frantic sheep cries reached Carl. Looking east, he saw part of the flock scattering in a terrified panic just across the creek. The large coydog raced among them.

Joe's gun sat just inside the door. Carl picked it up. The feel of the cool wooden stock made him sick to his stomach. He tightened his grip. He owed it to Joe to protect the sheep. It was just a wild animal, not a man. He'd done much worse. He could do this. He just hadn't expected God to test him so soon.

He tightened his grip on the gun. He wouldn't let Joe down.

He made Duncan stay inside and closed the door, then he sprinted toward the sheep in trouble. The frenzied bleating of a lamb guided him to his target. The coydog had a lamb down at the edge of the creek. He saw Carl and stood over a struggling lamb with his head lowered and his teeth bared.

Carl raised the gun and sighted along the barrel. His finger curled over the trigger but he couldn't pull it. He drew a shaky breath and lowered the gun.

He couldn't do it. Not even to save the lambs. He couldn't take a life, even that of a predator.

He stepped closer and yelled. The coydog flinched, but stood his ground.

"I won't kill you, but maybe you'll think twice about going after sheep again."

Carl sighted carefully. He let out a sharp whistle. The

coydog lifted its head and perked its ears. Carl fired. The bullet hit the rocks in front of the animal, peppering him with bits of stone. He yelped and took off, shaking his head as he ran.

Carl crossed the creek and hurried to the downed lamb. It struggled weakly as he picked it up. Its injuries appeared superficial. It was suffering from exhaustion and shock as much as anything. "Joe's going to have to invest in a few more guard animals to keep the rest of the flock safe in case that big fellow didn't get the message. I've heard llamas make excellent guardians."

He picked up the lamb and cuddled it close. "Don't worry, little one. I reckon Lizzie will have you fixed up in no time. I only pray that I can mend the harm I've caused her."

He started toward the house with long, sure strides. He had wounded Lizzie as surely as the coydog had wounded the lamb in his arms. If it took him the rest of his life, he would show Lizzie how sorry he was. If she gave him a second chance, he'd never shut her out of his life again.

Surrounded by her sisters and her grandfather, Lizzie sat at the kitchen table and tried to gather up the pieces of her broken heart. Jenna and Christina had gone to the inn in Hopes Springs for the night. They would travel home tomorrow.

Lizzie propped her chin on her hand. "I've made such a mess of things."

Clara laid a hand on Lizzie's shoulder. "You were trying to help."

"My interference didn't heal a family breach. It has driven Carl farther from those who love him." Including her.

"He'll come back," Joe said. "In time, he'll see that you meant well. Everyone makes mistakes."

"I've made more than my share lately." She looked out the window as the lights of a car swept into the yard and stopped.

"Now who is here?" Joe asked.

"I don't know. I don't recognize the car. It's not the one that brought Jenna earlier."

She had her answer a moment later when her uncle Morris and Rufus Kuhns stormed through the door.

Chapter Fifteen

"Onkel, what are you doing here?" Lizzie demanded. Her voice trembled with fright.

"I have come to take you and your wayward sisters home. How dare you defy me in this fashion?"

"How did you find us?" Betsy had tears in her eyes.

"Lizzie wrote a letter to you, but you were already gone. When I saw the postmark, I knew you had come here. You will be disciplined for this disrespect of your elder. Get your things and get in the car." He slapped a thick wooden yardstick on the table, making them all jump.

Rufus advanced on Clara. She shrank back in fear. He raised his fist and shook it at her. "You have made me the laughingstock of our community. You will come back and wed me." He grabbed her arm.

"*Nee,* I will not."

He struck her across the face. The women shrieked in outrage. Lizzie grabbed Clara and moved to put her own body between Rufus and his victim. "Leave her be."

Joe rose to his feet. "Get out of my house."

Morris pushed him back into his chair. Joe fell and grimaced with pain.

Rufus glared at Lizzie. "I'll teach you to interfere between a man and his betrothed." He raised his hand to hit her. She cowered before him.

"Enough!"

Everyone turned to see Carl in the doorway. He held a rifle in one hand and a lamb in the other.

Rufus eyed the gun. "This is a family matter, Englisch. It's none of your concern."

Carl set the gun against the wall and ignored the red-faced man. "Are you all right, Joe?"

"Right as rain. What's the matter with my wee woolly?"

Carl spoke softly to Lizzie. "He's been mauled. I need your help. We need to clean his wounds."

She was frightened, but his calm words gave her courage. She moved away from Rufus, pulling Clara with her. "Go get some towels, Clara. Greta, put some water on the stove to heat. Betsy, would you fix some milk for him? It's in the barn. We need to get fluids into him."

"Sure." Betsy started for the front door.

Morris smacked the table with his stick again. Clara and Betsy flinched, but Clara went up the stairs and Betsy went out the front door.

Lizzie heard Duncan barking in the distance and hoped he would stay away. Her uncle wasn't fond of dogs.

She took the lamb from Carl's arms. It cried pitifully. "It's all right. We'll fix you up."

"Stop what you're doing and get your things. We're leaving," Morris shouted.

Lizzie looked into Carl's serene eyes. "I think he may need stitches."

"You know best. Should we take him to the vet?"

Rufus and Morris exchanged puzzled looks. Lizzie knew they weren't used to being ignored.

"Obey me, you ungrateful child." Morris raised his stick and stepped toward Lizzie.

She closed her eyes and tried to shelter the lamb. She knew what was coming. Suddenly, Carl's arms were around her, shielding her. She felt him flinch with each blow her uncle struck, but he never made a sound.

A crash followed by screaming made her open her eyes. Duncan had charged through the mesh of the screen door and launched himself at Morris. Her uncle fell in his attempt to evade the dog. He was lying on the floor, trying to beat the dog off and screaming for Rufus to help him.

Rufus aimed a kick at Duncan. The dog easily evaded it and turned his attention to his new attacker. Darting in and out, he sought a hold on Rufus's leg and found it. Rufus hollered in pain.

Morris saw his chance and made a dash for the front door. Duncan, seeing his prey on the run, charged after him. Morris barely made it out, slamming the wooden door behind him. Rufus made a limping run for the back door. Carl spoke quickly. "Leave it, Duncan. Down."

The dog dropped to the floor and lay panting as he watched his master for his next command. Outside, the car engine sprang to life and the vehicle roared up the lane. Lizzie had to wonder what the Englisch driver must think of the evening's events.

She realized she was still in Carl's arms. She relaxed against his chest and drew several shuddering breaths. He lifted her chin with his hand and gazed at her face. "Are you all right?"

"I should be asking you that."

A tender smile pulled at the corner of his mouth. "At this moment, I've never been better in my life."

"Then maybe I can stay here a little longer?"

He pulled her close and tucked her against him. "You definitely should."

The front door flew open. Betsy stood there gasping for breath. Clara ventured down the stairs with towels in her arms and Greta moved to Joe's side to check on him. He patted her hand. "I'm fine."

Carl smiled at Betsy. "Duncan was shut in my hut. How did he get out?"

She was still panting. "I opened the door for him because it sounded like he wanted out. Onkel Morris doesn't like dogs. I thought they should meet."

Clara dropped to her knees to hug Duncan. "You are a wunderbar guard dog."

He wagged his tail happily. Joe said, "Bacon for that boy tonight for sure."

Everyone began to talk at once except Lizzie. She was content to rest in Carl's arms. She never wanted to move. It seemed her grandfather finally noticed.

He cleared his throat loudly. "We should get that lamb fixed up."

Carl reluctantly released her as her sisters came to take the lamb from her. He said, "We need to talk."

She pressed a hand to his cheek. "The past is over and done. It need never be mentioned again."

He flicked her nose with one finger. "It's not the past I want to talk about, Lizzie Barkman."

"After this baby is fixed up, would you care to drive into town with me? I need to see Jenna and Christina. I have a lot of explaining and apologizing to do. To all of you."

Naomi Wadler greeted them with some surprise as they came into the lobby of the inn. Carl approached the counter. "My sister Jenna King is staying here. Would you let her know that I'd like a word with her?"

"She and Christina are in the café. I'll show you the way. How is Joe getting along?"

"Fine. You should come by for a visit," Carl said with a slight smile for her.

She blushed. "I'll do just that. Tell him I'll be by with some canned goods on Sunday."

He and Lizzie followed her to the café doors. Lizzie caught his arm. "If you want to speak to your sister alone, I can wait in the lobby."

He covered her hand and gave her a reassuring squeeze. "I want you by my side."

The smile she gave him warmed his heart. The Lord had truly blessed him when He brought her into his life.

They found Jenna and Christina seated in a booth in the corner. Christina saw him first and jumped up to hug him. "Kondoo Mtu, I thought I would never see you again."

Lizzie took a step to the side as he hugged the child in return. Jenna looked uncertain about what her response should be. He kept one arm around Christina, but he held out his free hand. Jenna scooted out of the booth and threw her arms around him.

He choked back the tears that threatened to keep him silent. "I'm sorry, Jenna. I'm so sorry for the hurt I've caused you and everyone. Can you forgive me?"

"All is forgiven. All is forgiven. Come home, Carl. We love you. We miss you so much."

He looked over Jenna's head at Lizzie. "I don't deserve such unselfish love."

"Yes, you do," Lizzie said softly.

He read in her eyes what she wanted to say. She loved him, too. Soon he would be able to tell her how he felt, that he loved her with his whole heart and soul. For now, he had to believe she could see his love for her shining in his eyes.

After everyone's tears were dried, Naomi brought them slices of pie and cups of coffee with a mug of hot chocolate for Christina.

Jenna took a sip of coffee and sniffed once. "What are your plans now, Carl?"

"I thought since you have already hired a driver that I would ride home with you."

"Mamm and Daed with be so happy to see you. It will be a wunderbar surprise."

"I'd like to see the bishop first thing and explain myself."

Jenny reached across the table and took his hand. "You know that he and everyone in the church will rejoice that you have returned."

"I know. The thing is, I'm not going to stay, Jenna. I'm coming back here."

She glanced between him and Lizzie, who was blushing bright red. "Although we will hate to lose you again so soon, I think everyone will be happy for you."

"I won't be happy," Christina said with a pout.

He ruffled her hair. "I'll come visit a lot. You'll come to visit me here, too."

"Can I feed the lambs again?"

They all chuckled. He nodded. "Sheep Man said you may always feed the lambs."

When they were finishing their pie, Naomi approached again with a large box in her arms. "Lizzie, I have something for you."

Lizzie's eyebrows shot up. "For me? What is it?"

Naomi laid the box on the table. "Open it and see."

Lifting the carton lid, Lizzie squealed in delight. "It's my mother's quilt!"

Naomi smiled at her. "The buyer thought you should have it back."

Lizzie's eyes narrowed as she met his gaze. "Carl, did you do this?"

He held up both hands. "I tried, but someone beat me to it."

"Who?" Lizzie looked at Naomi.

"I promised not to tell."

Lizzie pulled the quilt from the box. "But it was so much money. I need to pay someone back. I can't accept such a gift."

Naomi fisted her hands on her hips. "You can and you will."

Lizzie's eyes narrowed again. "Naomi, did you do this? Do I owe you money?"

"*Nee,* it wasn't me. I'm just glad the quilt is back where it belongs. Your mother made it as a wedding gift for you. I know, and the buyer knows, that she would want you to have it. She would be so pleased that you used it to help your sisters find a safe home."

Lizzie held the quilt to her face and closed her eyes. "Please give my thanks to the buyer. I can't believe it came back to me."

Naomi patted Carl's shoulder and winked at him. "Now all that is needed is a wedding."

On the last Sunday in April, the congregation of Bishop Zook found itself in for a few surprises.

Carl had gone to meet privately with the bishop a few days before. Lizzie didn't know what they talked about, but she knew Carl planned to join their church if the congregation would ultimately accept him. It had to be a unanimous vote of all baptized members, so she knew Carl would be under close scrutiny for the next few months.

He looked very handsome in his dark coat and flat-topped black felt hat. He spent a lot of time running his hands up and down his suspenders. She could tell he wasn't used to them after wearing jeans for more than four years. There were a lot of surprised looks when the bishop introduced him after the service.

Faith Lapp had delivered a healthy seven-pound baby girl the week before. She brought her to church for the first time and everyone, including the Barkman girls, took turns admiring her. Adrian stayed by his wife's side, playing the role of proud papa with ease.

Lizzie, like everyone else, dropped her jaw when the banns between her grandfather and Naomi Wadler were read aloud by the bishop as the last item of the morning. She turned to her sisters. They all shrugged. None of them knew anything about it. Joseph, in his usually abrupt manner, left early after church and avoided a ton of questions. Naomi climbed into his buggy with him and they drove off, leaving people to speculate wildly on their whirlwind romance.

Only Sally Yoder said, "I knew something was up between them all along."

Later that afternoon, when Lizzie and her sisters arrived home in Carl's new buggy, they all piled out and rushed into the house.

Naomi held up a hand to forestall their questions. "He was supposed to tell you."

Joe looked defensive. "The time never seemed right. It's my decision to wed. If it doesn't suit any of you, too bad."

The sisters surrounded him with hugs and best wishes.

No one objected to having a new grandmother in the family.

After supper that night, Carl asked Lizzie to come for a buggy ride with him. Her heart raced as she agreed.

They had been careful to keep things low-key during his transition from an Englisch to an Amish sheepherder. His presentation to the church was the next-to-last step on his road back to the faith of his heart. It opened the way for him to court Lizzie without damaging her reputation.

Carl drove them out to the lake. It was an old stone quarry that had filled with water a century before. It was a favorite fishing spot for some of the locals, but they had the place to themselves that evening. They got out of the buggy and found a large flat rock to sit on by the water. Lizzie got up and threw a half dozen stones into the lake to ease her jitters.

Carl rested back on his elbows and watched her. "Can I ask you a question, Lizzie?"

"Of course." She came to sit beside him.

"On the night your uncle showed up, what did you think when I walked in with a gun in my hand?"

"I saw the gun and lamb at the same time. I thought you had been out protecting the flock from the coydog."

He studied her intently. "You didn't think I would use the gun?"

"On my uncle? *Nee,* that never crossed my mind. Can I ask you a question?"

"Sure."

She hesitated a moment. "Did you shoot the coydog?"

"*Nee,* I could not."

She grinned with relief. "He hasn't been back. I'm grateful for that."

"I found out who owns him."

"Did you? Who does he belong to?"

"Our postman."

"He's the mailman's dog?" Lizzie laughed.

"He and his son stopped in to buy a club lamb a few days ago. He had the coydog with him. He said the boy wanted the dog to get used to sheep so he wouldn't bother the one they took home."

"Oh, dear. Did you tell them that he can't be trusted around the lamb?"

"I had to tell them he's been killing our sheep. They offered to pay for all the damages. They felt bad about it, especially the boy. Joe wouldn't take their money."

"He's too happy these days to worry about money."

"Naomi is making a new man of him, that's for sure."

"Speaking of new men, you look very Plain in your new suit."

"I am a new Plain man, and I'm in love with a beautiful Plain woman." Carl leaned close and Lizzie knew he was about to kiss her. She had never wanted anything more.

His lips touched hers with incredible gentleness, a featherlight caress. It wasn't enough. She cupped his cheek with her hand. To her delight, he deepened the kiss. Joy clutched her heart and stole her breath away. She had been waiting a lifetime for this moment and she didn't even know it.

He pulled her closer. Her arms circled his neck. The sweet softness of his lips moved away from her mouth. He kissed her cheek and then drew away. Lizzie wasn't ready to let him go. She would never be ready to let him go.

"I love you, Lizzie," he murmured softly into her ear. "You have made me whole again. I was broken, and you found a way to mend me. I lived a life of despair, ashamed of what I had done. I thought I was beyond help. And then you came into my life and I saw hope."

"I love you, too, darling, but it is God that has made us both whole."

"And the two shall become as one. I never understood the true meaning of that until this very moment."

He kissed her temple. "Will you marry me, Lizzie Barkman?"

Lizzie had never felt so cherished. The wonder of his love was almost impossible to comprehend. This man, who had seen so much of the world, wanted her to be his wife. Emotion choked her. She couldn't speak.

He drew back slightly to gaze at her face. "Am I rushing you? Please, say something."

"Can't you hear my heart shouting *yes?*"

"No, for mine is beating so hard that I can't hear anything."

"Yes, Carl King. I will marry you."

Suddenly, he lifted her off her feet and swung her around, making her squeal with delight.

"I love you, Lizzie. I love you. I love you. I will never get tired of saying that."

When he stopped spinning, her feet touched the ground again. She gazed into his eyes. "And I will never grow tired of hearing it. I can't believe this is real. I'm afraid that I'm dreaming."

"Shall I pinch you?"

"Don't you dare."

"Then I will simply have to kiss you again. If I may?"

She put her hands on his chest. "You may. For as often and as long as you would like once we're married."

"Then say it will be soon."

"November will be soon enough."

He growled and pulled her snugly against him. "November seems an eternity from now."

She wavered. "It does, doesn't it?"

"I think we should have a June wedding."

"June will be too soon, but I think October will be about right."

He leaned close. "As you wish, but this is the last kiss you will get until our wedding day."

She gave him a saucy smile. "Then you had better make it a good one."

He proceeded to show her just how wonderful a kiss could be.

* * * * *

Dear Reader,

I have never worked or lived on a sheep farm. I grew up with cattle and horses. We did briefly own a sheep when I was a child, but my father sold Snowball before I grew attached to him. I do remember trying to ride him, with unhappy consequences that required bandages—for me, not for the sheep. Maybe that was why Dad sold him.

As I began to research this story, I was privileged to meet a shepherdess who is also named Pat. She and her husband operate a sheep farm near where I grew up. Pat provided me with a wealth of information about sheep and about shepherds. I met her guard dogs, her herding dogs, her guard llama and her guard donkey. Sounds like quite a menagerie, doesn't it?

My visit occurred during the lambing season. There were lambs galore with brightly painted numbers on their backs to keep them with the correct mothers. I loved how the older lambs ran and played with each other. They were charming to watch. As I listened to Pat describe what the lambing season entailed, I was in awe. I hope I have conveyed even a fraction of the work that goes into a successful sheep operation.

In writing this book, my thoughts often turned to my Good Shepherd. The One who looks after all of us, protecting us from harm, gathering in the lost souls, never giving up on those under His care. I can't count the number of times the twenty-third psalm ran through my mind.

The Lord is my shepherd; I shall not want. He maketh me to lie down in green pastures: he leadeth me beside the still waters. He restoreth my soul: he leadeth me in the paths of righteousness for his name's sake. Yea, though I walk through the valley of the shadow of death, I will fear no evil: for thou art with me; thy rod and thy staff they comfort me. Thou preparest a table before me in the presence of mine enemies: thou anointest my head with oil; my cup runneth over. Surely goodness and mercy shall follow me all the days of my life: and I will dwell in the house of the Lord for ever.

To my mind, it is one of the most beautiful prayers of the Bible. Keep it in your heart as I keep it in mine.

Blessings to you and yours,

Patricia Davids

Questions for Discussion

1. Carl King was a man tortured by a mistake in his past, yet he was unable to ask for forgiveness. What keeps us from seeking forgiveness for our mistakes?

2. We can sympathize with Carl's actions in defense of a child, but he believed he made the wrong decision in that split second. Is the taking of a human life ever justifiable?

3. Lizzie Barkman showed remarkable courage by setting out alone to seek her grandfather's help rather than accepting her sister's fate. Do you know a woman who has done something heroic for her family or others?

4. Family relationships can be tricky. Joseph Shetler believed his daughter would not want him to interfere in the lives of his granddaughters. Was he right in that assumption? Why do you feel he was right or wrong?

5. The Amish practice of shunning has become fodder for popular fiction. Did you learn anything new about this aspect of the Amish in this book? What was it?

6. Shunning may be called "tough love" by the non-Amish. It is hard to turn away from someone you love when they have done something wrong. Should we grant forgiveness without seeing signs of repentance? Why or why not?

7. Joe went against the rules of his Amish faith when he allowed Carl to stay and work on his farm. What reasons do you believe he had for bending the rules?

8. No two Amish congregations are exactly alike. Are you familiar with any Amish in real life? What puzzles you about their lifestyle?

9. What aspects do you enjoy about the fictional town and people of Hope Springs, Ohio?

10. What aspects of Amish fiction in general do you enjoy?

11. Jesus is often called the Good Shepherd. In what ways do the characters in this story mirror the life Jesus calls us to lead?

12. Carl was separated from his faith for a time in his life. Has there been a time when you or someone you know felt separated from God? How was that breach healed?

13. Are there characters from this book or a previous book in the Brides of Amish Country series that you would like to see more of? Which ones and why?

14. What part of this story did you enjoy the most and why?

15. What part of this book did you enjoy the least and why?

COMING NEXT MONTH FROM
Love Inspired®

Available April 15, 2014

HER UNLIKELY COWBOY
Cowboys of Sunrise Ranch
by Debra Clopton
Widow Suzie Kent needs help dealing with her troubled teenage son. Can tough sheriff Tucker McDermott prove he's the perfect man for the job?

JEDIDIAH'S BRIDE
Lancaster County Weddings
by Rebecca Kertz
When Jedidiah Lapp saves her brothers' lives, Sarah Mast quickly falls for the kind, strong hero. But when he must return to his own community, will they ever meet again?

NORTH COUNTRY MOM
Northern Lights
by Lois Richer
Alicia Featherstone never thought she'd have a family of her own. But she can see a future with former detective Jack Campbell and his adorable daughter...if she can make peace with her past.

LOVING THE LAWMAN
Kirkwood Lake
by Ruth Logan Herne
She vowed she'd never fall for another lawman, but when widow Gianna Costanza meets handsome deputy sheriff Seth Campbell, he could be the man she breaks her promise for.

THE FIREMAN FINDS A WIFE
Cedar Springs
by Felicia Mason
Summer Spencer knows it's risky to fall for a man with a dangerous job. But how can she resist falling for charming firefighter Cameron Jackson when he's melting her heart?

FOREVER HER HERO
by Belle Calhoune
Coast Guard hero Sawyer Trask has loved his childhood friend Ava for as long as he can remember. Will their second chance at love be destroyed by a painful secret?

_____

LOOK FOR THESE AND OTHER LOVE INSPIRED BOOKS WHEREVER BOOKS ARE SOLD, INCLUDING MOST BOOKSTORES, SUPERMARKETS, DISCOUNT STORES AND DRUGSTORES.

LICNM0414

REQUEST YOUR FREE BOOKS!

2 FREE INSPIRATIONAL NOVELS
PLUS 2
FREE
MYSTERY GIFTS

Love Inspired®

YES! Please send me 2 FREE Love Inspired® novels and my 2 FREE mystery gifts (gifts are worth about $10). After receiving them, if I don't wish to receive any more books, I can return the shipping statement marked "cancel." If I don't cancel, I will receive 6 brand-new novels every month and be billed just $4.74 per book in the U.S. or $5.24 per book in Canada. That's a saving of at least 21% off the cover price. It's quite a bargain! Shipping and handling is just 50¢ per book in the U.S. and 75¢ per book in Canada.* I understand that accepting the 2 free books and gifts places me under no obligation to buy anything. I can always return a shipment and cancel at any time. Even if I never buy another book, the two free books and gifts are mine to keep forever.

105/305 IDN F47Y

Name _____ (PLEASE PRINT)

Address _____ Apt. #

City _____ State/Prov. _____ Zip/Postal Code

Signature (if under 18, a parent or guardian must sign)

Mail to the **Harlequin**® Reader Service:
IN U.S.A.: P.O. Box 1867, Buffalo, NY 14240-1867
IN CANADA: P.O. Box 609, Fort Erie, Ontario L2A 5X3

**Are you a subscriber to Love Inspired books
and want to receive the larger-print edition?
Call 1-800-873-8635 or visit www.ReaderService.com.**

* Terms and prices subject to change without notice. Prices do not include applicable taxes. Sales tax applicable in N.Y. Canadian residents will be charged applicable taxes. Offer not valid in Quebec. This offer is limited to one order per household. Not valid for current subscribers to Love Inspired books. All orders subject to credit approval. Credit or debit balances in a customer's account(s) may be offset by any other outstanding balance owed by or to the customer. Please allow 4 to 6 weeks for delivery. Offer available while quantities last.

Your Privacy—The Harlequin® Reader Service is committed to protecting your privacy. Our Privacy Policy is available online at www.ReaderService.com or upon request from the Harlequin Reader Service.

We make a portion of our mailing list available to reputable third parties that offer products we believe may interest you. If you prefer that we not exchange your name with third parties, or if you wish to clarify or modify your communication preferences, please visit us at www.ReaderService.com/consumerchoice or write to us at Harlequin Reader Service Preference Service, P.O. Box 9062, Buffalo, NY 14269. Include your complete name and address.

LI13R

SPECIAL EXCERPT FROM

Love Inspired

*Widowed mom Suzie Kent is desperate to help her
troubled son. Is her only hope the man she blames for her
husband's death?*

*Read on for a preview of
HER UNLIKELY COWBOY by Debra Clopton,
Book #3 in the SUNRISE RANCH series.*

"Suzie Kent. It's good to see you." Tucker McDermott's
eyes crinkled around the edges, but concern stamped his
expression, as if he knew the dismay shooting through her.

Her breath had flown from her lungs and she had no
words as she looked into the face of the man she held responsible for her husband's death.

The man she was also counting on to help her save her son.

The man she wasn't prepared to see, though she'd just
driven three hours with a moving van and plans to live on
Sunrise Ranch, the ranch his family owned and operated.

Her world tilted as she realized whose clean, tangy
aftershave was teasing her senses and whose unbelievably
intense gaze had her insides suddenly rioting. His hair was
jet-black and his skin deeply tanned, making his deep blue
eyes startling in their intensity.

"Tucker," she managed, hoping her voice didn't wobble.

Moving to Dew Drop, Texas, to Tucker's family's Sunrise
Ranch, asking for his help, had taken everything she had
left emotionally—and that hadn't been much, since her
husband had given his life in the line of duty for fellow
marine Tucker two years earlier.

Tucker grimaced, trying to keep most of his weight off Suzie and Abe, but his hip clearly hurt.

"Thank y'all for helping me," he said, his gaze snagging on hers again and holding. "I've got it from here, though." He pulled one arm from around her and the other from around her son, Abe.

"Are you sure?" she asked, even though she wanted to step away from him in the worst way. "Do we need to get you to your vehicle?

Tucker limped a few painful steps away from them. "I'm okay," he said gruffly. "It'll just take a few minutes for the throbbing to go away." He glanced ruefully at the donkeys on the road. "What a mess. They act like they own the road."

Abe chuckled. "They sure took you out."

"By the way, I'm Tucker McDermott. I was a friend of your dad's and I owe him my life. He was an amazing man." Tucker cleared his throat. "I'm glad you've come to Dew Drop. And the boys of Sunrise Ranch are looking forward to meeting you."

Will this cowboy heal her family—and her heart?

Pick up HER UNLIKELY COWBOY to find out.
Available May 2014
wherever Love Inspired® Books are sold.